# Stone spun down into the vortex of white water...

Just when he knew he was dead, that he had reached the bottom and there was no farther to go, he felt something pulling at him. For a split second, in his half-delirious drowning state he thought it was giant snakes, a childhood fear suddenly dredged up out of the terror of imminent termination. He struck out at the grasping snakes trying to dislodge them from his body.

Suddenly he was sucking in air and realized he wasn't even in the water but up on land and that he could breathe. But when he opened his eyes Stone saw the meanest-looking bunch of dudes he had ever laid eyes on, and every broken-toothed, scarred face was streaked with garish stripes of reds, greens, and yellows in sharp, nasty-looking patterns. It was an Indian war party. And Martin Stone was General Custer.

**Also by
Craig Sargent**

The Last Ranger
The Savage Stronghold
The Madman's Mansion
The Rabid Brigadier
The War Weapons
The Warlord's Revenge
The Vile Village

**Published by
POPULAR LIBRARY**

# THE CUTTHROAT CANNIBALS

## CRAIG SARGENT

**POPULAR LIBRARY**

An Imprint of Warner Books, Inc.

A Warner Communications Company

POPULAR LIBRARY EDITION

Copyright © 1988 by Warner Books, Inc.
All rights reserved.

Popular Library® and the fanciful P design are registered
trademarks of Warner Books, Inc.

Popular Library books are published by
Warner Books, Inc.
666 Fifth Avenue
New York, N.Y. 10103

 A Warner Communications Company

Printed in the United States of America

First Printing: July, 1988

10  9  8  7  6  5  4  3  2  1

# CHAPTER

# One

THE strangest thing about an avalanche is how quiet it is at first. A few pebbles bounce noiselessly down a slope, or a little ridge of snow from high on a mountain skitters down with no more sound than that of the wind through trees. It is almost like a dream, at first. A thin veil of rocks or snow fills the distance, then the gray curtain seems to grow and expand in every direction like a stain spreading across a piece of fabric. A mist shoots up violently from the ground and blots out the sky above. And just before the moving wall of matter—the twisting maelstrom of dirt and snow and twigs and dead animals that it has already consumed—strikes, the sound comes. And it comes with a terrible roar.

Martin Stone looked up startled as he pulled back on the throttle of his immense Harley 1200cc. A deafening noise seemed to envelop his every cell as if a blanket of pure sound were descending on him. He was totally confused for a second as the sound seemed to come from everywhere, from all around him. But it took only another second for his ears to pinpoint the truth. Then he saw it—the wall of death coming down like the smashing hand of a jealous god. There was no way out.

"Jesus, mother of Mary," Stone muttered through suddenly chattering teeth as he saw the waterfall of ice roaring down the four-thousand-foot mountain slope straight toward him. In his stark and sudden terror Stone did not realize that the statement he had just uttered was both biologically and theologically impossible.

Behind him there was a sudden low growl from the ninety-pound brown-and-white pit bull that lay clamped around the leather seat like an oyster around a pearl. The furry head of the canine lifted up and its eyes opened, instantly growing to the size of well-cooked eggs as the animal saw that it was about to die. But if the avalanche had the slightest bit of mercy in its thundering soul, it was that it wasn't going to give them both a hell of a lot of time to worry about it all.

Even as Stone ripped back on the Electraglide's throttle so hard that the Harley did a wheelie for a second, the wall of white and gray came down the steep slope like a tidal wave, fifty feet of sheer grinding annihilation. A sound emerged from the very core of the thing, as if the gods were roaring out in pain. Then, before he could tear a hundred feet along the deer path he had been driving down, hitting nearly sixty miles per hour in three seconds, the avalanche slammed into the motorcycle like a million fists made of steel.

Stone didn't know where the hell he was. In a split second he was out of the normal world and into a grinding hell in which he was twisting around, as if inside a spin dryer. Somehow he hung onto the bars, gripping at the sides of the Harley with his thighs. The avalanche lifted the bike right up onto the crest of the crashing wall of white. He was riding a fucking motorcycle surfboard on an avalanche wave. For a second he heard the shrill squeals of the dog behind him even above the deafening roar of total destruction. Then the thunder grew so loud he couldn't hear a damned thing.

Suddenly he could see through the grinding mist that rose up everywhere around him. And he wished he couldn't. Because riding at the very forward curl of a fifty-foot wall of crashing ice and heading straight toward a wide ravine ahead was not exactly Martin Stone's primo choice of how to spend a crisp Rocky Mountain morning. But then, the avalanche didn't give a shit about his feelings. Avalanches were like that.

Martin Stone knew he was going to die. And in a paradoxical way, because he *knew* he was going to die, he relaxed deep in his guts. He'd known it was coming. That was for damned sure. From the moment he'd left his father's ultramodern mountain bunker, Stone had been living on borrowed time. When the major had been killed by a heart attack and Stone had taken the rest of the family out into the New America—after five years of living behind granite mountain walls—it had begun. First his mother had been raped, mutilated, and killed by bikers within just hours. Stone had been beaten and left for dead, only inches from death. Now it was only him and his sister, April. And God knew what would happen to her or what was happening to her right now, because he wasn't going to be able to continue on his quest to find and rescue her. Sorry sis, gotta die.

He seemed to hang up there, suspended on the very forward lip of the great avalanche as if it were the Perfect Wave that all surfers spend their lives searching for. He must have been a good sixty feet in the air as the avalanche just grew even larger, like an expanding conglomerate, as it shot down the slope. Somehow the bike was caught in the surging tip of the fall and just kept plowing ahead, almost as if it were riding the thing of its own free will. The sky and the mountains flashed all around him as the Harley bucked and shook, rose and fell ten yards at a time. Stone's face and eyes were peppered with a cutting ice as the spray shot out like a geyser from the rushing waterfall of frozen debris. It was bizarrely beautiful with the sun still coming up and the sky all orange and glowing like the face of a Halloween pumpkin, the clouds shining with a luminescent blue. It was beautiful if you liked dying.

Suddenly everything seemed to speed up into overdrive as the great wave accelerated. The whole world was spinning topsy-turvy, blue and orange and white, until Stone thought he would vomit from the loss of gravity as he didn't even

know which way was up. He felt as if he were on the edge
of losing his sanity.

He heard the dog let out a piercing yowl behind him and
realized he had forgotten that there even was a dog behind
him. Suddenly the bike with both of them hanging onto it
like laundry onto a clothesline was sucked down into the
lower regions of the pounding snow. The snow blotted out
the sky like dirt being shoveled over a corpse's eyes, and in
an instant Stone was being buffeted every which way. He
suddenly was ripped right off the bike and thrown around
like a broken doll, his arms and legs snapping out wildly in
all directions, so powerful was the centrifugal motion created by the crashing ice and snow.

Stone took a deep breath but sucked in only thick slush
that filled his lungs with a terrible freezing wetness. Then he
was tumbling end over end and could feel an incredible
pressure—as if he was being crushed—coming from every
side. The pressure increased until he could feel his lungs
being squeezed in, constricted as if he were in the grips of a
python. It was over. He couldn't hold his fucking breath any
longer, and Stone knew when he opened his lips the next
time it would be the last time. Ice, not sweet air, would fill
his throat and lungs.

He ripped open his jaws and gasped, and air came pouring
in. Stone threw his eyelids apart and saw in a flash that he
was falling. There was a river below, wide, with foaming
brown water rushing along fast. The avalanche had reached
the ravine and tossed him right over. Stone's eyes searched
madly in the air as snow followed down in sheets all around
him. For a moment he thought he saw the dog scampering
wildly in the air as if trying to swim. But then it vanished in
the mists that were rising as the snow hit the rapids below.

Stone felt the presence of something just above him and
quickly arched his neck to see the Harley, perhaps twenty
feet up and hurtling down like a black missile on his tail. He
ripped his head down again. The river was coming up at him
like a brown fist but it was worse than that. He was coming
down not into the water but onto the jagged rocks lining the

shore like rows of waiting teeth. Somehow he spread out his arms and legs and quickly twisted his hips again and again, trying to pull himself back out over the water. If the gods had been messing with him they suddenly gave him a break, for a moment anyway. A huge load of snow over the ravine suddenly hit the river and sent up a cloud of mist and spray that caught Stone full in his spread-out chest and legs. It pushed him with the kick of a mule about twenty feet further out from shore. But he didn't have time to say any thank you's.

For the water was there, ripping up at him in a brown blur. He slammed into the rushing river and felt a jolt of intense pain rip through his body as if he had just been stuck with a cattle prod. After all, he had fallen nearly two hundred feet. Stone's brain tumbled into complete darkness as the sheer impact of the fall was too much for his nervous system to handle. It just went on overload for a few seconds, the timer fuse blowing out and then resetting as his body reached the end of its downward trajectory about twenty feet deep in the water. The current plus the natural buoyancy of his body ripped him back up again and he popped to the river's angry surface like the bobber on a fishing line. Stone's lungs filled deeply again just as his head cleared the water and the breath brought him back to half-consciousness.

But, even in his semistupor, Stone could see that he was just out of the frying pan and into the flood. He was floating along in the center of the swollen river, which was even wider than it had seemed from the air, and rougher too. The river was a churning brown ocean capped with whiteheads and waves slapping wildly against one another like crowds of overenthusiastic theatergoers. For just a moment his whole body was turned around in the current and, looking back, he saw his Harley. Broken into pieces as if a bomb had gone off inside it, it was lying spread out among the rocks, flames licking up from its burst fuel tanks. Well, I won't be needing it anyway, Stone thought cynically even as the water playfully snapped him back around front again, as if it had been showing him his past and now was going to show him his future.

It didn't look too fucking bright. Ahead, the river got, if anything, more swollen and rough. He could see branches poking up everywhere and carcasses floating all around, already bloated from the intake of water so they looked as if they'd been dead for days instead of hours. Stone tried desperately to clear his fogged senses. He felt like he'd been Mickey Finned—everything was in a fog, a haze of wet grayness. It was as if the curtain that draped over death's very entrance was falling over him, a veil from another world.

"Son of a bitch," Stone suddenly spat out along with a mouthful of water. *I ain't gonna go that fucking easily*, he thought angrily. If he had survived the fall maybe he could survive the crushing river ahead. On second thought maybe not, Stone realized, as his waterlogged clothes began dragging him back under again. He could feel himself going down, and try as he might there wasn't a damned thing he could do to stop it. The saturated pants and jacket felt as if they weighed a thousand pounds, and his own diminished strength, about that of a three-year-old, didn't help matters any. Not when he was being carried downriver through swirling currents and whipping foam playing with him as if he were a rubber duckie in a tub. And even as he frantically tried to pull off the combat jacket he was wearing, Stone felt himself going down.

Then the sky, the light, disappeared from his eyes and he went under, just another unlucky creature swallowed up by the flood-swollen river. He sank down a foot or so beneath the river's surface, and for just a second he could see the dimness of the sky above him through the water. It was like looking through the distorting lens of a broken camera. And just for that instant he swore he saw a skull, dark and mocking, staring down at him. Then he was sucked down and his own skull was filled with a terrible bursting pain.

\* \* \*

From out of the jaws of the grinding river a demonic-looking face appeared, like some sort of creature from mythologies past. It swam with rapid strokes of its four legs, which paddled away beneath the surface like wheels on a Mississippi riverboat. And through the currents, through the swirling whirlpools that dragged animal corpses down into the river's black stomach, through the branches and whole trees that tore downriver smashing everything in their path, the pit bull swam, its eyes fixed unerringly on the spot where it had just seen Stone disappear. His head bobbed up again for a flash, and even from the thirty or so yards that still separated them the dog could see that Stone was in bad shape, his eyes closed, face blue. Then the head disappeared and this time it didn't come up again.

Like a duck heading for home the dog paddled even harder, shooting sideways through the rushing river. Suddenly it reached the spot where Stone had gone down and without faltering in its motion curved its body and headed straight down into the water, like some sort of furred dolphin. It swam frantically back and forth a few yards beneath the surface searching for him, but could find nothing in the mud-swirling nether regions of the rapids. Then suddenly it saw him, caught in a swift rip current about six feet down and being pulled fast. The canine shot in that direction, pushing with every ounce of its strength. And even with that it barely moved an inch or two at a time. It seemed that the animal would never reach him, and it felt its lungs screaming for air. But it knew that if it rose up it would never see the sucker again.

With a final surge it suddenly became caught in the same current that was pulling Stone. The dog shot forward and slammed right into his chest. His arms and legs were just flopping around like something dead, but the dog didn't wait to carry out any examinations. It opened its jaws filled with teeth capable of snapping through steel plate. The jaws closed around Stone's collar and the animal pulled with everything it had. Up it rose through the murky waters, rising as though from a nightmare. Somehow it broke surface and then headed toward the closer shore, about fifty feet off. The going was incredibly rough, for the pit bull was trying to deny the very forces of nature. It snorted wildly hardly able to breathe with the heavy package in its mouth. And Stone, completely unconscious and turning half purple from the water he had swallowed, was no help at all. He was more like a corpse.

Then just as it seemed that the animal couldn't go another inch, its eyes nearly popping from the Odyssean exertions of its task—a sandbar suddenly came into view poking out from the bank about twenty feet off. The dog gave a final lunge, pushing forward with all four feet at the same instant, and, with Stone's shirt buried in its mouth, it slid forward up onto the bank and out of the river's deadly grasp. The animal pulled forward, never so happy to have been on solid ground in its life. It dragged Stone, its four paws sinking deep into the watery sand, and after about twenty seconds had pulled him a good forty feet back, off of the sandbar and onto the safety of the rocky shore. The dog sat back breathing hard, its tongue hanging out of its mouth, its whole body trembling, chest rising and falling rapidly as it filled its lungs again and again with the delicious oxygen. And as it greedily sucked in air it stared hard at its provider. But Stone wasn't moving. Not a twitch.

## CHAPTER

# Two

S TONE didn't move for many minutes as the dog stared down at him, its eyes locked on his face like a priest contemplating the beyond. Without realizing it, the animal had done perhaps the only thing that could have possibly made a difference to the half-drowned Stone—it had set him down on his front, on his chest and stomach. The pressure of his own body slowly forced the water in his lungs to ooze out so that a small trickle of muddy liquid dripped from between his lips and down onto the sand just an inch below his face, which was turned sideways on the rocks. It was as if gravity itself was giving Stone artificial respiration as the liquid just kept being squeezed from the saturated lungs until nearly a quart had come out.

Suddenly Stone coughed, a hacking, throat-wrenching sound that made even the dog feel a pain rush through its neck. He sucked in a mouthful of sand on the intake. Sputtering and spitting, he pushed his arms down hard. They felt as if they were made of rubber, but were able to generate enough energy to roll him over. For a few seconds Stone thought he was still underwater, and he clawed at the air like an enemy as his lips drank in the cold oxygen. But then as he realized he was in fact able to breathe, his eyes shot open, and he saw that he was alive and that a silver dollar of a sun was weakly cutting down through a misty cloud cover above. To the side of the sun a huge furred face, with a long pink tongue lolling out of it, hovered over Stone's face, a drool of saliva pouring down right onto his nose.

"Christ, dog, don't drown me all over again—okay?" Stone grunted, realizing even as he spoke that the damned dog was alive too. Things were turning out a little better than he had expected. He raised himself up onto his elbows, still lying in the sand, and looked back toward the river. A deep trail led from the edge of the sandbank about fifty feet away. The animal had dragged him all the way out of the river. Excaliber had saved his life. There was no question about it.

"Sorry about that, dog," Stone muttered sheepishly as the canine stared back, its head tilted to the side, looking at him a little concerned. How the Chow Boy could have survived all this time without the assistance of the pit bull was beyond the creature's comprehension.

Stone tried to move and a fire shot up and down his right leg.

"Shit," he half screamed out as his whole head filled with explosions of color and pain. He looked down at the leg and saw that it was bleeding profusely. He realized he had a compound fracture—the thigh bone of his right leg was actually poking through the purple skin, like an ivory snake emerging from its fleshy burrow. Stone thought he was going to be sick for a second and he gagged, turning his head to the side and coughing up another glass or so of the brown river water. After that he felt a little more clear-headed as it appeared he had cleaned out most of the muck he had taken in.

Slowly it dawned on him just what had happened and where he was. The bike was gone. Damn! He had depended on the thing. It had been with him since he left the bunker. With its speed and formidable armory of weapons it had been a mini warwagon. It would be difficult to survive without it. But if he ever got out of this alive, it was just barely conceivable that he might be able to construct another back at the bunker—just barely. Stone snickered at his morbid thoughts as he lay there in the middle of nowhere. He thought he heard a growl in the grove of trees that stood about a hundred feet off and reached down for his Ruger .44-cal. It was gone, as was the Uzi. He'd lost everything. Excaliber let out his own guttural growl back toward the source of their would-be visitor, and whatever was out there seemed to disappear—at least for the moment.

Stone tried to rise and instantly collapsed. Aside from still feeling as weak as a newborn, explosions of mind-wrenching pain shot up and down his right leg and his backbone at his slightest attempt to get up on the appendage. And here he was stuck with no medical equipment in the most remote area of the entire territory. Not that anyone out there would do anything except kill him and perhaps eat him if he were to be found. Stone made a silent reminder to say his prayers more often, because something up there sure as hell was pissed off at one puny mortal being named Martin Stone.

The river seemed to be slowly edging toward them as the floodwaters rose another notch or two. It was absolutely filled with debris now, animals, torn trees, fish swirling around the rushing waters in dead schools, spinning around like propellers as they followed one another down through the foaming pathways. Well, he was alive, and he might as well stay that way, Stone decided with a snort as he tried to ignore the burning slivers of sensation that were running along his entire right side, threatening to send his brain back into dreamland from the sheer intensity of the jolts. He had to move fast before the whole fucking scene fell completely apart. The dog was something else, but he wasn't a surgeon.

"Dog," Stone said, coughing up more dark spittle. "Dog, you listening?" Stone asked, as the animal stood just feet away staring straight at him with an amused expression. "You better be listening cause I need your damned help." Stone snorted again and looked away for a second. Something inside him hated the idea that the dog was so necessary for his survival. It was supposed to be man who aided the dumb but loyal beast, not the other way round.

"My leg," Stone said, grimacing fiercely as he dragged himself up on one elbow. Even that was a torturous visit to Painland as any movement with any part of his body made the inch or two of bone that protruded from his thigh dig around like a kitchen spoon stirring up the bloody soup a little more. There was no way he could travel yards, let alone the hundreds of miles back to the bunker, without drastically altering his physical state. And he'd better work fast, for the blood was starting to flow a little quicker around the edges of the pierced flesh. A red stream already coated his whole calf and the small rocks and sand beneath him. Lying in a puddle of his own blood was quite depressing.

He leaned his head back, ignoring the pain that demanded his attention, and surveyed the shore that the dog had pulled him onto. There was another forty feet or so of rock-littered sand, then a tree line filled with fir and spruce. Thick groves of the towering trees ran for perhaps another fifty yards at most, then stopped at the base of the granite mountain that

ran alongside the river. The towering wall was impossibly
high, blotting out three quarters of the sky above so that just
a long twisting highway of blue and puffy white wriggled by
overhead. The cliffs were thousands of feet high, virtually
straight up at ninety-degree angles to the earth in many
spots. He'd need pinions and ropes—ten thousand dollars'
worth of mountain-climbing equipment—and two good legs
to have even a chance to get out of there.

Stone could feel his heart quickening as adrenaline flowed
into him like liquor. "Calm down, you asshole—don't
panic," he half shouted, startling the dog, which jumped
backwards in the air, rising up nearly a foot off the ground
as it thought he was yelling at it. Stone chuckled at the sight
of the canine as its hair stood on end and its eyes suddenly
expanded to nearly double their size. Then it hit the dirt
about a yard away and relaxed instantly when it saw Stone
laughing and realized that it hadn't done anything wrong,
hadn't broken one of the many incomprehensible rules of the
Chow Man.

And with the laughter came the first release of tension he
had had since being caught up in the avalanche. When he
stopped Stone found he could think just a little more clearly.
What would the major have done? Stone tried to visualize
his old man getting stuck in exactly the same predicament
somewhere in North Vietnam or Cambodia or any of the
hundred places he'd dealt in his trade with the ultraspecial
forces of the Rangers. Well, number one, his father wouldn't
have let himself get stuck in such a situation. But what if he
did, Stone demanded of himself. The first thing he'd do is
fix his fucking leg.

He scouted around the tree line and spotted broken
branches lying around their bases. Some appeared fairly
long and straight—perfect for making a splint.

"Dog," Stone said, suddenly growing a little hopeful in
spite of himself as he began wondering if maybe he did have
a snowball's chance in hell of getting out of this whole fiasco.

"Over there, see that branch? Branch, dog, you hear me?

BRANCH!" Stone pleaded desperately with the animal, imploring it to understand what he was saying. The animal looked at him with a curious expression, tilting its head back and forth as if trying to comprehend the meaning of the moving lips and the squawking sounds emerging from them.

"Play dog, play!" Stone shouted encouragingly, making a throwing motion with his hand toward the spot where pieces of branch lay scattered around from a lightning strike that had slammed into a grove of Colorado spruce a week before. "Get stick," Stone grimaced, throwing his arm forward again, trying to make the animal think he had actually heaved something.

Whether Excaliber believed the dreadful charade or not Stone would never know, but it took off like a rocket in the direction he had pointed. The pit bull flew about thirty yards until it reached the branch pile. It stood there staring back at Stone and barked a few times as if confused.

"Pick up a fucking branch, don't play dumb with me, dog," Stone half screamed across the shoreline, wincing with pain at the end of the command. The dog, as if tired of farting around, reached down and picked up the biggest one it could find and clamped its teeth down around it. It tore back to Stone dragging the ten-foot-long, five-inch-thick piece of broken tree limb along with it. With the dog's powerful jaws and legs it was easy going for a load that would have made a man stagger a little. Excaliber pulled the branch right up to Stone and let it fall to the rock-strewn sand.

"Good boy," Stone said enthusiastically. The damned animal could have been on the fucking Johnny Carson show in the old days, no question about it. He leaned over, trying to ignore the waves of exquisite torture that ran along his spinal cord as he touched the wood. It was strong but too thick for a splint. He'd be like a walking table with a leg this thick.

"Listen dog," Stone said, looking over at the animal that was only a foot or so from his face, its tongue hanging far out as drool rolled down it and onto the ground. "You did good, real good," Stone said, nodding his head. "Better than any other dog in the entire fucking state could have done, you can bet your bone on that." He looked closely at the animal's inscrutable almond-shaped eyes to see if it was listening. But as usual the canine remained as poker-faced as some hardened card shark sitting in a broken-down shack of a bar in the middle of the wastelands.

"You did good, dog, but you got to do better," Stone said, his smile vanishing as he felt a little flood of blood spill out from the protruding bone like a fountain of red to set off the ivory. "I need another one. Thinner." He made motions with his hands as he touched at the thick branch, indicating that he needed something about half as wide. The animal looked on in utter puzzlement as if it didn't have the foggiest idea what Stone was talking about. He was like an Eskimo trying to communicate with a Watusi—a lot of flailing around with hands, babytalked words, and not a bit of understanding.

At last, as the dog just didn't seem to be picking up on his philosophical subtleties, Stone made the throwing motion with his hand again. Following the arch of his hand, as if it were trying to calculate the trajectory that a piece of wood would have made, the animal took off like a racehorse from the starting gate. It was hauling ass so fast by the time it reached the branch graveyard that it couldn't stop in time and skidded right into them sideways rolling wildly about, its paws pumping in all directions. Stone lowered his head for a moment and shook it, glad for the dog's sake that there weren't any other mammals around to witness the animal's grace. But what it lacked in smoothness it sure as hell made up for in innate animal wisdom. For after nosing around in the pile that extended like a set of fallen pick-up sticks for about thirty feet, it at last chose one. Setting it firmly in its glistening teeth it tore back to Stone. And even from the distance he could see immediately that it was perfect, exactly half the size of the first in both length and width.

"Dog, you've outdone yourself," Stone said, looking at the animal with almost a hint of fear on his face, as it had been so accurate about what he had needed. "Excaliber, I'll ask you once and then never again," Stone said, staring intensely at the creature as it let its treasure fall right next to

Stone's leg. "Do you understand every fucking word I've ever said? Is this all some giant headgame and you're really Einstein with fur, just playing with me?" The animal's only response was to slap out the wet tongue like a reptile whipping out at an insect. The tongue swept right up over its eyes and then across its whole muzzle, then pulled back into the white-and-brown face, which looked back at Stone with the perfect emptiness of the void.

The branch was about two inches thick and green. The stuff was tough and wouldn't give even under a lot of pressure. Stone reached for his custom Randall Bowie knife, but of course it, like everything else, was gone. He cursed himself for not even thinking about how he was going to slice the damned thing up. Even at his best, Stone knew it would be a bitch to rip the branch apart barehanded.

"Shit," Stone muttered, so depressed for a moment that even his physical pain diminished next to the fact that without any supplies or equipment whatsoever human beings weren't one fucking inch above the animal world. Perhaps they were even below it. For tools were what defined men, and Stone had none. Suddenly Excaliber's pointed canines caught his attention. The dog could bite through one of these if he felt like it. Stone had seen the creature chomp through tables, beds, metal pipes, things a damned sight tougher than this piece of wood, and leave them in splinters.

"Dog, time for another little favor," Stone said sweetly. He held the branch out, his fists about a foot apart on it, and pushed the wood up against the animal's nose. But the pit bull pulled away quickly, sputtering and spitting out the branch. "Don't fuck with me now," Stone yelled maniacally. "I'm not in the mood. You've got teeth—now bite!" As if acting out a game of charades again, Stone snapped his mouth open and closed so his teeth clattered loudly against one another. The animal stepped back another foot or two, just to make sure that the pink creature hadn't gone completely bananas, even rabid perhaps. For the dog had seen other rabid dogs and skunks slam their teeth together like that. But then seeing that the Chow Boy wasn't about to actually launch himself at the dog, Excaliber walked forward again, sniffing at the strong scent of the green cracked wood.

It licked gingerly at the surface, getting a taste of bittersweet sap that it seemed to like as it licked at the oozing crack in the branch a few times.

"Don't lick—bite," Stone half screamed, knowing his energy was fading. The sun would set in hours, and if he didn't get out of this situation, he would be up shit creek with a frozen paddle. "Bite, bite!" Stone demanded, again snapping his mouth so hard that it made his teeth hurt. Suddenly the dog seemed to get the message, for it barked and moved into a half crouch, its muscles all tensed and coiled as if to say the bullshit was over. Making sure that Stone's hands holding the fallen tree limb were far enough apart, the bull terrier opened its mouth to the widest extension possible. Then with a blurred snap like the jaws of a shark, it closed them hard onto the wood.

Stone felt the shudder of the branch in his hands and nearly fell forward from the sheer ferocity of the attack. It was like a killer shark's sudden, ruthless move on its prey— the same blinding motion, the same snap of the head when contact was made to give an extra rocket boost of power to the blow. And Stone wondered for a crazy split second if the damn dog was related somewhere way way back to sharks of the prehistoric world, predators of immense size that would make even today's watery monsters seem like mere guppies. Pit bulls the size of dinosaurs—that was all the world needed, Stone mused as he held on for dear life to the shaking branch.

Excaliber's teeth ripped into the green wood, tearing it into paperlike shreds. Once, twice, three times he pulled his jaws a few inches open and then slammed the guillotine shut again. With over 2,000 pounds of pressure per square inch exerted, the most of any canine in the world, it didn't take long. The second bite did it and the third severed any of the remaining green silky tendrils that clung to one another. Stone held both the severed pieces up and, selecting the stronger and straighter half, held that one up again for the dog to do its thing with. Within seconds he had two perfect pieces. Reaching down, Stone ripped back at his blood-soaked tattered pants.

It wasn't a pretty sight. Looking at it, he felt the bile rise up in his guts. There's something about seeing one's own flesh ripped and pierced deeply that makes most men feel a little funny inside. The bone was poking right out, cracked as cleanly as the branch the dog had just done his beaver act on. During the avalanche or the fall into the river the leg had just snapped right in two like a turkey bone at a Thanksgiving dinner. He could still feel it, all the veins and arteries were working, but there was a sense of incompletion without the straightness of the bone. For a moment Stone felt what it would be like to lose a limb, and he didn't like the sensation at all.

He gritted his teeth and pulled on the leg, forcing it with a screaming effort back into the flesh. The broken edges disappeared back inside like worms descending into their holes. A spurt of blood from the pressure squirted up from the wound right into his face, coloring his vision red for a few moments. Stone didn't hold back on the scream that echoed back and forth, up and down the granite mountain walls. The pit bull squealed and bucked up in the air again, obviously a trifle on edge from the day's events.

But Stone knew that was only the half of it. With the bone back inside, he again took a deep breath and then extended the leg out as far as he could, trying to push it into some kind of anatomical symmetry with itself so it wouldn't jut out at a bizarre angle halfway down his thigh. And through the curtain of pain, he could feel the two parts of bone join and mesh, and his leg felt right for a second. Stone stopped and fell backwards, cringing in pain but keeping one hand firmly clamped down on the set leg so it wouldn't jerk free again.

After about a minute, the volcano seemed to settle down in his skull. Stone sat up and checked out the wound. The blood was still oozing out, but at least the leg looked fairly

straight, the way he liked it. Stone undid his belt with some
difficulty and then placed both three-foot-long sticks along
each side of the leg. When it was all placed together about
as well as he was going to get it, he wrapped the belt around
wood and leg and tightened it closed. The belt acted not only
as the tie for the branches but as a sort of tourniquet, depending on how tight he made it. Stone reminded himself to
loosen the thing every twenty minutes or so. Or as the major
had once said to him, when describing gangrene, "the flesh
starts turning purple then actually green, and the pus is so
thick that if you squeeze it, it comes out like a rotten banana
from beneath the stinking flesh." Gangrene was not something Stone was looking to add to his list of life experiences.

Taking the other half of the branch the dog had brought—
this section was about three inches thick and five feet long
—Stone put his weight on it and, pushing with all his arm
strength, somehow rose up so he was standing. *There, that's
better*, Stone thought to himself, trying to trick himself into
feeling positive. He looked around, up and down the river,
then along the banks on each side and the towering mountain
walls that formed the river valley, searching for a way out.
The river, the sheer slopes, the raging foam, the early evening sky starting to lose its daytime luster, all possessed a
certain dark beauty. But try as he might Martin Stone
couldn't see a single avenue of escape.

# CHAPTER

# Three

STONE hobbled around on his makeshift splint and crutch, testing out just how functional his leg was. And the answer was: not very. He felt as if he had been put through a meat grinder twice and then sewn back together again by somebody who had taken lessons from Dr. Frankenstein's gardener. But the leg seemed to hold up, though a jolt of electricity ricocheted up and down his nervous system every time he put the slightest bit of weight on it. And the bleeding was slowing as a dark coagulation began forming on the outer skin.

The dog trotted happily along beside Stone. Now that Stone was up and about doubtless in no time he'd have them both out of there and off to a nice hot meal. No doubt about it. Already the canine, whose stomach was feeling quite empty after all the rescue operations, began visualizing meat and slabs of gravy-soaked bread, and saliva began flowing from between the opened jaws in a waterfall of anticipation.

"Come on dog, out of the way," Stone said, mock smacking the creature with his hand for it kept walking right in front of him, making him half trip. He didn't know what the hell kept rustling up a storm back in the thick but not very deep groves of trees. And he didn't want to. Without his weapons—the pistols or the Bowie—he was a sitting duck, a sitting injured duck, that just about anything bigger than a groundhog wouldn't have a hell of a lot of trouble taking out. The dog would have to be his defense and offense for

the moment. And for one of the few times in their short but
fiery relationship Stone was glad the animal was such a
tough, brawling son of a bitch.

With Excaliber leading the way as a sort of furred mine-
sweeper and Stone screaming out curses telling everything in
the neighborhood with teeth or claws to get the fuck out of
there, they made their way about ten yards into the dense
thickets. Stone heard the sounds of things scuttling away a
few yards off, but whatever was making the noise remained
out of sight, which was just fine with Stone. The pit bull let
out a little huff of air or a small growl every few seconds as
its head turned back and forth surveying the shadows for
danger

Stone walked through the mini forest right up to the base
of the mountain wall that loomed overhead. He didn't even
know what the hell he was looking for, but he sure wasn't
finding it. The rock peaks seemed impossibly high. Already
Stone was starting to feel claustrophobic. He had to lean his
head all the way back even to see the tops of the damned
rock giants, which seemed to look down from all around
him, laughing from their imperious heights. He was like a
little squashed ant. And he knew it.

The ribbon of light overhead that was the sky began dim-
ming like a bulb about to blow. A stiff wind suddenly spat
down from the north, sweeping back and forth from mountain to mountain, sending leaves flying from each bank, depositing sheets of rotting vegetation into the churning liquid.
Stone's clothes were sopping wet and he knew that, with the
temperature drop that would come when night fell, he was
going to be one frozen human popsicle. Even his blood
would harden like ice. Things weren't exactly getting better.
Stone searched himself again for the third time, praying that
in his still dizzy state he'd overlooked something. But that
wasn't the case. There wasn't a firemaking implement in his
pockets. Not even a single match. And he wasn't exactly the
Boy Scout type. Besides, rubbing two sticks together for the
next two hours would take every last bit of strength he had.

"When in Rome, do as the fucking Romans do," Stone

addressed the dog, as he sat down against a tree and began taking off his boots and pants, cutting up over the wounded leg to allow the splints to pull through. The dog rested on one side and watched with fascination as Stone stripped down buck naked. Not wearing clothes itself, it didn't quite understand what they were, but it knew that the Chow Boy didn't usually start ripping them off in the middle of nowhere. The canine once again began wondering about the sanity of its master with some apprehension.

"Oh fuck off, dog, don't look at me like that," Stone exclaimed, slapping his shirt out at the pit bull's head. "Never seen a naked man before, for Christ's sake?" Stone managed to remove all his garments from his battered body and, standing up, balancing on his green wood crutch, hung them on the low branches of a nearby white spruce. He looked around almost as if expecting a crowd to be watching this entire absurd procedure. But not a soul was out there except for the pit bull, which gave him a most curious glance.

"Pal, someday, if we ever get out of this, I'd like to get me an electric razor," Stone said, addressing the canine with a waving finger. "And shave every last hair off that stinking body. Then we'll see just who the hell smirks, and who slinks off like a snake in their nakedness." As Stone spoke, gusting breezes came in with the cooling evening, and the clothes were whipped around in the air like store signs in a hurricane.

Stone sat down again taking deep breaths. It was pitiful how tired he was from just that much effort. He was beginning to feel like he was never going to get out. But Stone cursed himself for his pessimism. He knew he needed every bit of his willpower and a belief that he *could* get the hell out of all this, or he wouldn't have a chance. As he undid the tourniquet around the leg to let the blood circulate through into the calf and foot, he thought how funny it was that the whole time he'd been out of the bunker, though he'd faced some tough bastards, he'd never really thought he was going to buy it. But now. . . . *SHUT UP! SHUT UP!* he commanded himself. He could almost see the major's face hovering over the mists of the river, watching him, watching how Stone survived. If he survived. If he had what it took.

Stone had firmly decided that he wasn't going to spend the night on the ground. He needed sleep so his body could heal even a little. But the idea of the various "Jaws" imitators out there nosing around his face wouldn't be exactly conducive to hitting dreamland. He rose up after airing out the leg for a few minutes and surveyed the trees around him. One big old sucker that looked as if it had been growing since the Pleistocene had three branches arching out at just about ninety-degree angles from the trunk about ten feet up. It was perfect. Reaching it was another matter.

"Dog, I'm going to need your help again," Stone said firmly, turning around. But the animal was already running off having a fine time of it. Stone didn't appreciate the pit bull's frolicking antics. A catastrophe was not the time or place to have fun. He'd have to talk to the mutt about that. The canine leaped around into the air, corkscrewing like some kind of deranged dolphin out of water. And then he raced back toward the river and went back into the water. You'd think the overactive beast would have had enough of the wet stuff after what they'd just been through, Stone thought with disgust. But as he saw a large silvery fish slither out of the animal's grasp, he realized Excaliber was trying to scrounge up dinner.

"Good luck," he snorted under his breath, having witnessed the animal's fish-catching endeavors before. He turned back to the tree he hoped to sleep in. Well, he'd obviously have to do it all himself since the dog wasn't going to be any help. Stark naked, somehow dragging back branches from the surrounding ground, Stone managed to get a bunch of them leaning against the tree so once he was up in it, he could just reach down, pull them up, and build a nice little condo in the sky. Simple, right? But then, as the wise man once said, "Theory is to reality, as dogs are to shit. That is, you step in it however much you try to avoid it."

Or something like that, though somehow he knew he'd gotten the saying a little mangled in translation.

He retrieved his clothes, which were actually wind dried, and spent a good half hour just getting them back on again. It was amazing, Stone realized as he struggled with even the simplest of tasks—like putting on his socks—how much one takes the most basic things for granted. Once he was fully dressed, Stone discovered that he couldn't even get up the damn tree. It might as well have been Mt. Everest, for, as much as he leaped up at it, grabbed at it, and kicked at it, he just couldn't get a grip.

At last he found a thick branch from among the ones he had gathered with enough smaller offshoots still on it that it created a crude ladder. Using this, he leaned up against the spruce, and scraping his arms and chest into reddened welts and bruises, somehow monkeyed his way up. He reached the three-branch intersection and, grabbing hold of a twisted piece of wood, pulled himself up. Breathing heavily, he surveyed the terrain around him with the first feeling of satisfaction he'd had since the whole fiasco began. At least he was safe for the night. Now he had to build his tree house.

Dragging up the long pieces of wood and lashing them together with some vines he had found was virtually impossible. There was room only for him up there, and manipulating the difficult-to-hold branches was frustrating.

"Oh Christ," Stone said at last, completely exasperated, as he shoved the five pieces he'd pulled up back down to the ground, where they banged together with dull thuds. He lay back against the hard bank and tried to find a comfortable position, which was difficult. But after about five minutes, using his jacket as a mattress, he found something approximating comfort, if not actually being it. Scarcely had his muscles begun relaxing when he heard loud barking at the base of the tree. Stone glanced down to see the dog with a huge, still flapping fish at his feet, posing happily in front of his prey, one paw on the long, gasping mountain trout,

like some tourist from the city here on summer vacation.
The animal looked up expectantly.

"Good boy," Stone laughed, as he felt his stomach growl.
He couldn't even remember the last time he'd eaten. There
had been supplies in the Harley—tins of chocolate, hard-
bread, emergency rations for a few days. God, he'd give his
right testicle for a fucking Spam sandwich right now. The pit
bull grabbed hold of the big fish, its scales a silvery orange
in the very last rays of the dying sun, which sank suddenly
away like a drowning man beneath the waves of night. Excaliber gripped the fish firmly in his jaws and then crunched
hard twice. The trout stopped moving. The dog leaned up
against the side of the tree and held the fish up toward
Stone, who was genuinely touched by the gesture.

"Son of a bitch, you are a decent little fucker, aren't you,"
Stone said, feeling a little misty-eyed that, though not a person in this whole fucked-up world seemed to like him (in
fact most were trying to kill him), this one waterlogged mutt
did care. "Thanks pal, I'm deeply touched," Stone said, as
the dog slid back down to the ground. "But not tonight.
Without fire I don't think I'd quite savor the taste of cold
raw fish. But go ahead man, eat it up. Do your goldfish
routine."

The pit bull did not have to be told to eat. It ripped into
the fish with a savage fury, taking down a good third of it
with a single immense snap of its jaws. The chewing
sounds, the bones crunching, the odor of fish that wafted up
to Stone got to his stomach like a rocket. It just growled and
growled even when he poked it and slapped at it to pipe
down. All that he could see in his mind were steaks and
fries, and all that was on the menu was ground-up raw fish.
Yet the more Stone tried to deny it the hungrier he became.
Sushi, he suddenly remembered eating Sushi in Denver.
*That* was raw fish. It was sliced thin of course, and marin-
ated in herbs and vinegar and God knew what weird Japa-
nese ceremonial voodoo juice, and cut up with swords and
chants. But still it was just plain ol' raw fucking fish. Right?

Stone leaned over the tree and saw the pit bull preparing

to launch itself at the main and meatier part of the fish, which it had been holding as the main course. "Hold it, you pig," Stone screamed down, waving his hand to ward the dog off. The thought of even this wretched dinner vanishing forever into the furred mouth was beyond his ability to cope. And in his sudden fear of going mealless Stone misjudged a little. His hand slipped free from its branch and suddenly, like a meteor falling from the black heavens, he tumbled out of his perch.

"Shiiiiiiiitttt!" he managed to squeak out as the ground came up at him. Fortunately for Stone, the landing site of his greed-induced fall was a thick bush a good five feet high. He slammed into the thing stomach first and felt the whole piece of vegetation give and half topple over. But it held him. Not a piece of his body even touched the ground. Extricating himself from the scratching bush, another dozen or so red welts across his face and arms, Stone managed to stand on one leg, leaning against the tree.

"Don't say a fucking word, dog," Stone snarled as the pit bull stood back about six feet, its eyes wide in terror when it saw Stone hurtling down.

"We share, right? Share," Stone said, leaning over and grabbing a whole eight-inch-long section of what looked like the tenderest part. He lifted the delicacy to his mouth and nearly gagged, for half-chewed fish, with dog saliva, dirt, and whatnot all over it was not the most pleasing thing he had ever had laid before him on a dining table. But his stomach made noises again, and Stone, vowing to have the damned thing removed if he ever had the chance, stuffed a big slab of fish into his mouth as if it was the last thing in the world he wanted to do.

It tasted like shit. Exactly as he expected. How they turned this stuff into food was beyond his wildest imagination. For the cold, wet, salty mess in his mouth was more like something that should be vomited out rather than taken in. But after the first bite stayed down—even after a minute —Stone chewed desultory munches from the trout carcass. The pit bull seemed to be having the time of its life, chomp-

ing hard, then throwing bits of fish in the air and catching
them, barking after each successful toss and catch, then
looking over at Stone.

"Chill out," Stone snarled. "I hate happy dogs. Didn't I
tell you that? So eat your fucking fish and look depressed,
like I do." The dog either didn't or wouldn't understand his
words and just kept munching away making loud sounds of
gratification every few seconds. Stone had eaten about a
dozen or so careful slow bites to make sure he avoided the
bones, when he heard it. It was very soft at first, just some
branches snapping in the now darkened woods covered with
a sheet of gray and black. Excaliber stopped his chewing too
and stood straight up, his ears cocking up into radarlike
dishes searching for the enemy.

They saw it at the same time—a large shape that
loomed about forty yards off, up on its hind legs. And
now he knew for sure that somebody up there hated his
goddamned guts. It was a grizzly! A monster, a good ten
feet as it stood up on legs the size of tree trunks. Black as
midnight with a thick glistening coat. It sniffed at the air,
its huge wet nose pumping in and out like a bellows. The
fish—shit, the damned carnivore had smelled the meal.
Stone threw the remnants of what he held in his hands
down and leaped to his feet, grabbing at his walking stick.
For an instant he looked toward the river, wondering if it
might be the best avenue of escape. But the bear was
already circling around in a slow curve, cutting off any
such retreat. The son of a bitch had been bred for tens of
thousands of years to know just what the hell it was doing
and just how to catch, and kill, prey.

Excaliber began growling, his ears flattening back, fur
bristling, but Stone called angrily to the dog as he backed
away toward the tree he had been lying in. "Get over here,
dog, over here, don't even *think* about messing with that
bastard or you're pit bull stew—you hear me?" The pit bull,
which had taken on dobermans, wolves, outlaws, even a
lion, knew he was outclassed. This thing had to weigh a ton.
It would be like attacking a tank. Backing off slowly, but

growling like a motherfucker just to show the huge carnivore, now about twenty yards off and closing fast, that he could fight the overgrown teddy bear if he wanted to, Excaliber moved back until he was right against the base of the tree.

"Now, come on," Stone screamed as he fumblingly erected the makeshift ladder he had made for himself earlier. He scrambled up the branch commanding himself to stay calm. But his heart didn't seem to want to listen as it pounded away inside.

Somehow, grunting with bursts of pain as he put any weight on the broken leg, Stone scrambled up the ladder and set himself on the ledge created by the conjoining branches of the tree. It wasn't going to be high enough—he could see that even as he looked back down. The fucking bear could stand this high. But it would just have to do because Stone wasn't going any higher.

"Come on, dog, dammit, jump, get up this thing," Stone screamed, looking down to where the dog had gone into hunting posture, lining up the approaching grizzly with its three-pointed stance—tail, shoulders, and nose all lined up straight at the creature's throat. The bear stopped for a minute as it came rumbling through the shrubbery about forty feet off. It stood up again to its full height. It was a monster. The ears of the beast were almost level with Stone, and suddenly his little tree house seemed like a joke.

As Excaliber saw the thing stand up, whatever vague thoughts the dog had been harboring about taking on the beast in a one-on-one quickly vanished like so many bloody bubbles in the wind. It turned and tore up the branch, scrambling along it like a monkey. Stone helped the dog get aboard on the juncture and kicked the ladder away—not that the bear needed it. He reached around behind him and found the stick he had left before, a good stout green thing about three inches thick and five feet or so long. It looked like a toothpick in his hands as his eyes caught the carnivore coming through the rye. The bear at first seemed more interested in the fish that had been left behind, perhaps knowing that its two treed friends weren't booking any flights to Hong Kong. It hardly bothered to look up at them, but nosed around in the dirt, snorting up pieces of trout and gulping them down in big bites without even chewing. Stone gulped as well, and heard Excaliber making a funny sound deep in his throat.

But as soon as the great beast had finished with its garbage collection, which took about five seconds, it focused its attention completely on the tree. It walked over on all fours, the great body rolling from side to side, so Stone could see the tremendous muscularity of the beast. Whoever said the animals were fat must have been insane. For the tree-sized predator looked like it had been taking body building courses, as sheets of muscle rippled through its legs and chest. And when it stopped, looked straight up, and opened its mouth with its rows of huge jagged teeth, Stone got a chance to see those too.

The bear suddenly heaved itself up on its back legs with a big grunt of energy, and the musky stench of the animal suddenly filled Stone's nostrils.

"Back, back," he screamed at the dog, which pulled itself up another six feet or so, scampering along a thick branch and into the higher needled foliage. Stone pulled himself up too, pushing off from the tree ledge with the stick. He found another little meeting point of two branches across from the pit bull, about seven feet above where he had been sitting. The bear seemed to take it all in stride. It set itself on its lower legs, shifted things around a little and then let out an ear-shattering roar.

It fixed its bottomless eyes right on Stone's as if to tell him, you can play all the tricks you want mister, but I'm going to eat you before the sun's up.

The massive right paw rose up through the branches pushing the smaller ones aside. Claws that looked a good eight inches long and sharp as icepicks at the tips, swept back and forth in the air just beneath Stone, catching the very bottom of the material of his pants. He was up a good fifteen feet and the bear was nearly able to reach him, as it soon would once it got hopping mad. Stone pulled his feet up as high as they would go, and catching one arm securely around a branch he slammed down with the green stick in his right hand. The shot was a good one and caught the grizzly square in the snout. And at that moment Martin Stone learned the one thing you can learn about fighting grizzly bears: go for their noses, the only vaguely vulnerable spot on the fur-coated beast, most of whose hide a spear couldn't penetrate.

Stone could see the shock in the great carnivore's eyes the moment the end of the stick slammed into the nostrils. The bear's eyes shot open as it let out a blood-curdling scream that promised pain and blood. Rivers of it. Then it really came after him. It was mad now. That much Stone had managed to accomplish. The huge head came snapping up out of the darkness. A fog of moonlight wafting down from the narrow sky that showed between the two towering mountain walls on each side of them suddenly lit up the grizzly, and Stone saw its gnashing jaws, saliva dripping out in torrents, the maddened demonic face growling in the middle of all that black fur.

He slammed the stick down again with every bit of strength he had, and the beast reeled but stayed on its feet. Yet again Stone cracked down, trying to force the creature back, to force it to submit to his will. At last after six, seven, eight strikes, the brute dropped down to the dirt with a roar that shook the mountain stillness as it echoed for miles. Birds normally asleep flew up from nearby trees at the sound. Excaliber let out a high-pitched counter scream, letting the bastard know that his side had only just begun to fight.

The bear walked around in a circle, shaking its head from side to side as if trying to clear its senses, like an old but formidable boxer a little punch-drunk from too many rounds. At last it seemed to get it together again and re-treated about forty feet. Then all two thousand pounds of the animal came charging in like a cavalry of murder. Stone steadied himself with every bit of strength remaining in his taut body. His teeth gritted like a wild man's as he timed the charging bear, holding his stick raised until the last possible second. The bear suddenly leaped up with all the strength of its thick hind legs. If a ball of fur as big as a small elephant can fly, then this black-pelted monstrosity was positively heading into orbit.

And Stone was waiting there to meet him. As if the black snout of the grizzly was the pitch that would save the Series, Stone swung down with every ounce of will and remaining power in his torn and fractured flesh. The combined forces of the bear's nearly unstoppable mass and the sharp focused stroke of the branch met with a bloody and noisy explosion. Stone felt the stick slammed out of his hand and he fell backward, barely catching himself on a thin branch before he went over and down onto the ground. He tensed himself waiting for the end, waiting for the crunch of those monster jaws. But nothing happened. And suddenly he heard the thing wailing up a storm as if it was having some kind of primal therapy session down below.

Stone swiveled his body around and stared down. The bear's whole face was mashed in, just a bloody porridge with more red pouring out every second. It didn't seem too bent on dinner anymore. It didn't seem bent on anything for that matter as it raced rapidly around about ten times in a tight little circle like a whirling dervish, and then shot forward in an absolutely straight line right toward the river, where it disappeared into the shadows of the trees. Stone heard splashing and then nothing.

# CHAPTER

# Four

STONE and the dog spent the entire night up in the tree, not being one hundred per cent sure that the bear wasn't about to make a reentry and a dramatic finale with their heads as trophies. Stone couldn't sleep a wink as every chirp, every rustling in the branches or on the ground sent surges of adrenaline into his system in quantities that could be bottled. Stone was annoyed to see that after about half an hour of growling and making general bestial noises from the far side of the tree the dog fell sound asleep. With his four legs draped over the branch, a good sixteen feet off the ground, the pit bull looked to Stone's fatigued eyes like nothing less than some mutant sloth, a genetic experiment that had gone terribly awry.

With the taste of rotting fish on his lips, his ass freezing from the cold night, his leg burning with an electric fire, and assorted other complaints too numerous to list, Stone had just about had it. His brain felt as if it was ready to erupt into spouting pink tissue from the events of the last twelve hours. He felt that he was in the front car on the Cyclone roller coaster at Coney Island, only he just kept going down.

At last as the sun began painting the ribbon of sky above the towering ridges of rock a dim blue, Stone allowed himself to feel just a trace of hope. With the dawn of a new day the eternal optimist in man bursts forth in absurd and ridiculous zeal as the first rays of light hit his retina and set his pineal and half a dozen other glands all working like mad. For if man wasn't a shit-eyed optimist and wishful buffoon

from the start he would have just turned around and walked
back into his cave and sealed himself off forever the first
time he ever saw what was awaiting him outside.

So Martin Stone raised his head toward the crazy dawn
speckled a hundred colors and vowed that he would make it.
*Fuck'em all*, he thought.

"Come on, dog," Stone yelled across the opposite branch.
Not an eyelid stirred. "Dog, we're on the road, we're outa
here, let's go." Not a quiver. Stone didn't want to start out
the day in a bad mood. He had already resolved to ignore his
leg, ignore everything bad, and concentrate on the positive.
But already he could feel his blood pressure rising, the
adrenaline flowing, teeth starting to grind. And he hadn't
been up five minutes yet.

"DOG!" Stone screamed, slamming out with the long
green stick that had done so well with the grizzly the night
before. The edge of the stick grazed the pit bull's shoulder
and that seemed to catch its attention. Enough to make it
raise its head lazily to see what fool was messing with it.
Once it saw that Stone had caught it looking up, it tried to
pull its head back down again fast, pretending that it was
actually asleep and that what had just happened, hadn't.

"Come on dog, don't be an idiot. I'm a human, I'm
smarter than you—I know you're awake. Now move it. We
gotta get going fast 'cause I don't want to spend the day
fending off that bear cub's mother, brother, sister, or uncle.
And if you weren't so damned lazy you'd think about it and
know that if we don't split its dog jerky time." Stone raised
the stick again, being in no mood for canine bullshit this
cold morning, the dew of the firs all around him dripping
down onto his face and hands as if he was in a mini rain
shower.

The dog jumped up, or tried to, sliding around on its
branch as it forgot for a moment that it was high up in a tree.
It yelped, not wanting to get struck again, though Stone
hadn't made a scratch on its thick and nearly impervious
hide. But in trying to avoid Stone's "motivator," the fighting
canine lost its grip, and with its paws flailing like mad it

slowly slid straight down the branch toward the lower junction. Letting out a shrill howl of hysteria, the animal built up speed as it shot down the six or so feet to the lower level. Its paws moved like pistons but not being quite equipped by nature for tree climbing, it just shot down the limb as if it was greased with oil. The dog slammed into the branch ledge and right across it, bolting out into the air. The pit bull kept swimming away on the insubstantial morning breeze as it shot out about eight feet. Then it looked down and saw that it was no longer traveling on tree.

The animal let out just about the most plaintive sound Stone had ever heard, then it dropped straight down. The distance, fortunately for the dog, was only about nine feet and it too, as Stone had done, landed in some low bushes, which cushioned its fall. Once Stone saw that aside from a wounded pride Excaliber was okay, he couldn't help but let out a smug laugh. The pit bull dragged itself from the greenery and looked up, giving Stone a mean scowl. It licked around at its legs and chest, making sure that everything was in working order. Seeing that it was, the pit bull sat down on its hindquarters and stared up at Stone as if asking what's taking you so long, asshole?

But having already taken the emergency exit once, Stone wasn't in any hurry to do it again. With his right leg all swollen up now and hurting even more than it did the day before, he took it slow as he maneuvered himself down the branch, onto the ledge and then down the tree. Without the ladder, which he had kicked away when the bear came visiting, Stone had to hang out from the branch and let himself drop, falling about five feet to the ground. Ordinarily the drop would have been no problem, but due to his fractured leg an explosion of pain ripped through his thigh when he hit dirt. He collapsed straight onto the ground and lay there groaning for nearly a minute.

When he finally managed to pull his mind back from the vat of pain it was flopping around in, Stone saw the pit bull staring at him. He swore the edges of its overtoothed mouth were curved back in something approximating a smirk. This whole avalanche experience had put the two of them in a fine fettle with each other.

But Stone quickly saw that he had worse things to worry about than interpersonal relations between the human and animal species. The ground was getting wet, very wet, like a fucking swamp. As soon as he came out of his daze he realized that his legs and chest and face for that matter were wet. He looked down. The ground was oozing with water, like a sponge. He pushed himself up and glanced quickly around. The earth all around him was like that. The river was continuing to rise. It hadn't abated at all. "Jesus Christ —the whole shoreline could be overrun," Stone muttered to himself, starting to get depressed again. He again looked up at the towering wall of granite and shook his head from side to side. There was no way in hell he'd even get ten feet up the side of that thing.

As he gathered his fallen walking stick, Stone saw that it was happening even faster than he had feared. A little wave of water came right across the ground from the river, sweeping toward them like an ocean. The dog jumped around in the inch-deep puddles that were quickly created. Stone made his way the fifty feet or so through the tree grove. He could see instantly as it came into view that the river was much rougher and higher than yesterday. Rains, snows further north, an old dam suddenly burst: something had happened. For the river was positively frothing today, foaming at the bit, like a horse, ten thousand horses, all galloping along, their heady white manes tossed back, their bubbling hooves pounding along with a thundering wet roar. And it was absolutely filled with debris—the corpses of numerous wildlife, birds, fish no longer swimming, and countless bushes and trees of every size, from tiny seedlings to great seventy- and eighty-foot giants that must have stood at the edges of the banks and had their roots weakened and undercut by the rushing currents. An armada of dead things.

"Great," Stone spat out through clenched teeth. The pain kept stabbing into him though he tried not to pay attention. There wasn't a hell of a lot he could do except grit his teeth.

In the unlikely event that he got out of all this he sure as hell was going to need a good orthodontist. But Stone knew the horrible truth was that his body would go way before his teeth would. They'd last a thousand years. If hundred-million-year-old dinosaur teeth had been dug up, it seemed likely that Martin Stone's own jaws might well find their way into the far future. Perhaps they would end up in a museum on some distant planet. The thought didn't give him much comfort, and he unconsciously felt around his choppers with his tongue to make sure they were still there.

Stone's brain whirred like a malfunctioning computer as he tried to figure out what the hell to do. He and the dog could stay here and climb the tallest tree they could find. But even then there were some giants coming downriver, and Stone had no guarantee that his particular tree would withstand them. And with the sky turning a dead silvery color and huge clouds rampaging down from Canada, it looked like there was going to be even more rain. As if the very skies were listening in on his most private fears, the clouds right above the long river canyon lit up with multiple volleys of lightning.

Then the sky opened up. It just poured down as if the pipes of heaven had exploded. Within seconds Stone could hardly see. And it didn't take a hell of a long time for the additional drops to add their power to the river. Within two minutes the water had swollen two inches. Within another minute another six. The cold liquid rushed in around Stone's ankles and knees as he stood about twenty-five feet from the churning rapids of the river, already over a hundred and fifty feet wide and getting bigger and meaner by the minute.

He heard a growl to his side and looked down to see that the pit bull had managed to snag an errant rainbow that had swum too close. He held it up toward Stone looking hopeful that perhaps they could stop and snack awhile.

"Dog, you don't have much sense for natural disasters, do you?" Stone said with a look of infinite disgust. "Spit it out," he commanded as he made a sudden decision and started walking toward the river's edge. "Because not only

are you not eating, but we're about to go for a little swim."
The dog spat out the fishy breakfast and trotted along at
Stone's heels. The water was up to its lower chest now so it
moved in great jumping strides more like a kangaroo than a
canine. Stone knew that he was insane, walking toward the
inferno of raging water instead of away from it. But he also
knew he didn't have a chance if he stayed. Once he was cut
off, up a tree, the waters would close in on him. This whole
section of shoreline would be completely under in minutes at
most. No, he was going to have to jump into the watery
volcano, try to make his way downriver to a shallower slope
that he could manage to climb up or at least sit it out on.
And pray real hard.

Stone cupped his hand over his eyes to try to keep out the
sheets of rain and sighted out along the river as it rushed by
him with all its multitudinous broken baggage. Even as he
stood on the rocky shore the water rose, inch by inevitable
inch. The rains—or the immediate cloudburst overhead at
any rate—seemed to abate momentarily though upriver it
poured down, adding tons of liquid to the flood every second. It was now or never. He could see a little better now
that the downpour dropped to a mist. He searched frantically
for any possible makeshift vessel he might take a little cruise
on.

There! Coming from around a bend in the river about a
quarter mile up, an immense tree a good seventy feet long,
perhaps six feet thick, covered with thick-leaved cushioned
branches. It was perfect. Something that big would push its
way right through other debris, maybe even be able to take
any rapids. Maybe.

"Come on, dog, I got us reservations on the *Queen Mary*,"
Stone said with a twisted smirk. He started into the water as
the pit bull yowled and looked at him incredulously as if to
say, "Wasn't it just yesterday that I saved your damned ass
and pulled you right up on this very shore—and now you
want to dive back in again?" But Stone wasn't arguing, just
swimming. He was suddenly in it—in the thick of the flood.
And it was a hell of a lot different being in it than it looked

from the waterlogged shore. For one thing, he was going completely in the wrong direction from the fucking tree. The currents were unbelievable. For about ten seconds Stone found himself whirled around like a top looking for a rock wall to crash into.

At last he found his bearings and managed to paddle back through the current at an angle heading toward the tree, now about twenty-five feet away but tearing by him. If he didn't get there soon the sucker would be gone. Suddenly he saw the pit bull thirty feet downriver, paddling like a beaver on speed toward the great fallen spruce. If the little ball of overgrown teeth could make it, Martin Stone was not going to let down the human race. He clenched his jaw and swam with everything he had, churning away in the water with his lean muscled arms toward the tree. Stone's wounded leg was almost useless, dragging in the water like an anchor of flesh. But he had been the captain of the swimming team when in college and his arms were strong. With his arms and his left leg, which could still kick, he was staying afloat.

*Okay asshole, this is the National Finals and you got ten feet to go to get the gold. So move it, boy,* Stone commanded himself, remembering the way coach Williamson had screamed at him. He surged forward, his arms feeling as if they were cast of molten lead. And just as the log swept past him, just as it lunged forward on its unstoppable path downriver disappearing like the caboose on a rickety old train, Stone grabbed hold of a branch with his right arm. His hand tightened like a vise around it and though it bent slightly, being only about six feet long, it held. The momentum of the huge tree barreling by at a good twenty miles per hour caught him and snapped him suddenly along with it, nearly breaking his grip. Stone careened through the water as if he were waterskiing on his face, his body creating a furrow behind the thing. Reaching deep inside Stone found a scrap of energy to pull his other arm around and up, and after a few seconds he was able to reach forward and latch on to another small branch.

It wasn't too difficult after that to pull himself up and onto

the huge nature-made boat. Once up on the leafy body of the
log, Stone pushed his way through the thick branches for
about ten feet, searching for the dog. Then he saw the pit
bull standing dead center on the log, balancing itself as the
thing buffeted it back and forth. As big as the damned tree
was, the currents were so powerful they were shaking the
thing around like it was just a big cork floating free.

The pit bull barked when it spotted Stone—it had thought
maybe he hadn't made it and wasn't feeling too happy about
that fact. And being the happy-go-lucky creature that it was
the fighting canine surged forward, forgetting that it was on
a floating log in the middle of a maelstrom—and nearly lost
its balance. Suddenly it was scampering away at the dark
wet bark like a test subject on a treadmill. Just as the animal
started sliding right down the side of the tree Stone moved
forward fast and threw out an arm, grabbing the creature by
one of its front legs. With one great heave he pulled the dog
up and onto the log, where it squealed with sudden fear and
had to do everything to control its own body not to twist
around and jump into the air in corkscrew motions as it often
did to release tension. But even a dog knows when to cool
it—when the fucking Red Sea is slamming in from every
side.

## CHAPTER

# Five

STONE had thought he and the pit bull were alone on
their little river ride. But he had scarcely settled into a
vaguely balanced position dead center on the tree when he
heard a sound emerging from the far end of the rising and

dropping tree as it sped through what felt like increasingly rough waters. It was hard to hear at first, like a whine, then like a buzz saw. And then as it emerged from the spiderweb of branches and its feline face came into view it made a screeching sound that sent fingernails clawing along Stone's backbone.

It was a mountain lion, one of the biggest sons of bitches Stone had ever seen, a good two hundred pounds if it weighed an ounce. And the animal had apparently never heard of sharing its toys when just a cub. No, this one seemed to want the whole fucking log to itself. And maybe, Stone saw as the golden-furred creature prowled slowly forward, moving low on its shoulders so the blades stuck up, its thick padded paws easily getting good traction on the slippery log, maybe it would get its way. It eyed the two recent arrivals from about thirty feet off and they eyed it back. Three different species all doing their own macho thing.

Excaliber suddenly let loose with a growl of challenge and went into his hunting point, lining up his body like a missile ready to launch itself straight at the predator's chest. The dog was not one to take any bullshit, from man or mountain lion.

"Easy, dog," Stone whispered out of the side of his mouth, not making any sudden movements. He knew the cat could be on them in the flash of an eye if it felt like it. It was playing with them. Cat and mouse, probably waiting to see if he had any weapons. But seeing no flash of steel that it knew could kill as its mate had been hunted down years before, the cougar came forward even more aggressively, picking up speed as if it was about to break into full charge.

Stone's eyes swept the tree around him for even the most primitive of weapons. There was nothing. "Son of a fucking—" Suddenly everything was a blur. Excaliber, sensing something in the killer's eyes, sprang right over Stone's head. The instant the pit bull shot into the air, the cat did the same, snarling and hissing. Stone was so hypnotized by the two balls of murderous fur flying toward each other that he froze in place, his mind numb as a rabbit looking into the headlights of an oncoming car. As it flew, its body stretched out to full magnificent length like a pelt about to be mounted on a trophy hunter's wall, the mountain cat opened its huge claws to take off the head of the animal that dared challenge it.

But though Excaliber was brave, it wasn't a fool. The first thing the animal ever did when confronted with another beast was to size the fucker up: give it a once-over and seek out its strengths and weaknesses. Having been in countless battles with countless kinds of creatures ranging from scorpion to gunslinger, the pit bull knew that in this particular fight it was outclassed as far as it came to brute strength. But not when it came to street smarts. For the dog had its own brand of martial arts when it came to meeting charging carnivores in midair.

Just as the claws of the big cat came swiping down out of the wet air like a fork searching for dinner, the pit bull somehow altered its flight path just inches from the mountain killer and dropped straight down onto the tree, landing on all fours. The cat sailed right over its prey and flew by, hissing and scratching at the air. Excaliber slammed its head back up, pushing at the same time with all four legs. The effect was as if the mountain lion had been propelled from a slingshot. It shot forward clawing at air and sailed right off the side of the tree and into the boiling waters. The furious predator splashed around in the frothing river in a rage of screeches and slashing claws. But by the time the killer got itself turned around and started toward the floating tree it was too late. Excaliber and Stone watched as the mountain cat paddled frantically behind them with an angry and forlorn look on its whiskered face—its fucking tree had not only been taken over by invaders, but it as well had been unceremoniously booted out. Just as the creature disappeared in the mists that rose above the river, Stone saw that it managed to crawl onto a smaller but nonetheless seaworthy log.

"Good dog," Stone said, staring back at the pit bull, which had turned and was looking at him with a most contented expression on its face, its tail wagging around like a cobra on acid.

"Son of a bitch, but you know how to fight, don't you, dog?" Stone said, leaning over and giving the sopping wet head a hard rub. "If this was the old days you could open a chain of self-defense franchises for dogs and make millions. Too bad you'll have to be resigned to a life of poverty like your traveling companion here." But if the animal had any monetary worries it kept them to itself, and just stared back at Stone with its unfathomable dark eyes, wagging its tail back and forth in simple but total zen joy at the defeat of its enemy.

Stone got to savor the removal of the mountain cat for only about thirty seconds, for suddenly they were in the midst of churning rapids that made the rough waters they had already been through look like a pond. Everywhere around them the world was white with foam and spitting funnels of water that smashed together rising ten, twenty feet into the air then crashing back down right on top of them. It was as if they were going through a car wash—one that was trying to kill them. Stone did all he could to hang on to the wet tree trunk as sheets of water came cascading over him. The tree rocked and jumped and flew around like a piece of balsa wood as even *its* tremendous weight was really just a tiny speck when it came to an angry mother nature and the power that flowed from even the merest of her temper tantrums.

Suddenly they hit a tremendous wave, a good thirty feet high. The entire spruce flew up out of the water, countless tons of it. For a split second Stone could see above the mist and spray on the surface of the river and ahead—to a washing machine of white water. Not that he was going to get to see much of it. For the tree came down like an elephant jumping into a tub and sent out a splash as high as the wave that had tossed it. Stone felt himself flying off the thing, just rising up as in a dream and gliding off at an angle. Then he was in the water and everything was just a blur of foam and mouthfuls of water and fear, terrible fear, for he didn't want to drown. Not this way, sucking in mouthfuls of water, the lungs exploding.

Blindly he swam, just trying to keep himself afloat, not even heading in any direction. Suddenly he felt himself pulled straight under as if a giant hand had grabbed him and yanked him right down. He was buffeted around at all crazy angles, pulled first this way and then that, like a child playing with his toy ship and constantly ripping neurotically at the controls as he couldn't make up his mind which direction he wanted the toy to go in.

Then he was nothing but animal consciousness, flailing around in a world where he couldn't grab hold of anything, which just spun and spun and seemed to pull him down ever deeper into a vortex of darkness. And just when he knew he was dead, that he had reached bottom and there was no further to go, Stone felt something pulling at him. For a split second, in his half-delirious drowning state, he thought it was giant snakes, a childhood fear suddenly dredged up out of the terrors of imminent termination. He struck out at the grasping snakes, trying to dislodge them from his body.

Suddenly he was sucking in air and realized he wasn't even in the water but up on land and that he could breathe. But when he opened his eyes Stone saw the meanest-looking bunch of dudes he had ever laid eyes on, and every broken-toothed, scarred face was streaked with garish stripes of reds, greens, and yellows in sharp, nasty-looking patterns. It was a fucking Indian war party. And Martin Stone was General Custer.

# CHAPTER

## Six

STONE half expected one of the Indian warriors to say, "Now you die, paleface." Instead, the nearest of the braves standing in a semicircle around him, with a face painted in jagged red and yellow dayglow stripes, spoke up.

"White asshole, you look like shit." The other Indians stared hard, their mouths twisted into grimaces within their warpainted faces. They were all powerful-looking men stripped to their waists in animal hide pants, carrying only traditional Indian weaponry—bows and tomahawks—though the latter were made from hammered-down meat cleavers, Stone noticed as his head began clearing slightly.

"You could say that again," Stone grinned, rubbing his head where he must have taken a hit from one of the rocks when he took his little water ride. "Did you . . . guys"—Stone faltered for a second, not sure what the hell to call them—"save me?"

"Save you?" The brave who stood above him looking down as if from a towering height laughed. "No, white man, we just pulled you from the river. Pulled you from one grave into another. You'll most likely die now that you've stumbled onto our world. That will be up to Chief Buffalo Breaker, he with fists that can kill buffalo, Hwanata—my father."

At least they weren't going to bleed him on the spot, Stone thought, though it was little enough comfort. From the way the half dozen or so men of bronzed muscle stared at him, their dark eyes peering through those nightmarish painted faces of stripes and jagged lines, with wolves and serpents drawn in brilliant colors all over their bodies, from the way those faces looked at him with purest malevolence in them as if they could imagine nothing more enjoyable than ripping his heart right out of his chest at that moment, it didn't look promising. But even savages have moral codes by which they live. Or at least these did.

"Sounds like fun," Stone said, trying to rise. Suddenly there was a commotion about fifty feet down the sandy shore and they all turned, reaching for various knives and tomahawks. An Indian that Stone hadn't seen was backing away from the water and toward the group surrounding Stone. And coming toward him walking in a crouch with its teeth snarling and its body so completely drenched with muddy water that it looked like some sort of aquatic rat that wasn't having very good luck was Excaliber. As the brave retreated, his red skin turning a much whiter shade, he reached for a long blade at his side. But somehow he didn't seem particularly interested in trying to use it. The dog looked like it had just jumped up from hell itself, so fierce were its almond eyes, absolutely bearing down on the Indian.

"Dog!" Stone screamed with something approaching joy. He hadn't even had time to wonder about the dog, and if he had, doubtless he would have been sure it was dead. But Wonderdog, albeit looking like refried shit, had made it through the watery gauntlet. The rest of the braves tried not to look uptight, keeping their lips as hard as cast iron, but in their flashing eyes Stone could see fear. For some reason the dog seemed to scare the shit out of them, way beyond its physical threat.

"That . . . your dog?" the brave who had been speaking to Stone asked, with a dash more respect suddenly in his eyes.

"Like I tell everyone," Stone smirked, "we travel together but he's his own animal." *To say the least,* he added under his breath. Excaliber kept coming forward in that low crouch like a wolf, as if ready to spring off those overmuscled legs at any second and launch right at the throat of the green-faced brave who, still walking backwards one careful and slow step at a time, had reached the rest of his band.

"Call him off, call him off," the chief's son demanded nervously as he too whipped out a long machetelike implement. "Don't want to have to kill." The brave seemed almost desperate, and Stone could see that Excaliber had some strange effect on the Indians way beyond his menacing stance. The steely frames and scarred bodies of the Indians attested to their toughness, but the quotient of stark fear in their eyes was more like what a man might have of a charging grizzly like the one Stone had faced, than of a dog. But perhaps he could use all this to his advantage. If only he knew what the hell was going on.

"Excaliber," Stone called out, slapping his hands together. The clap caught the pit bull's attention like a bomb, and the dog's ears ripped around toward the source of the sound.

The instant the animal saw Stone its whole body relaxed, and it rose up higher on all fours and trotted happily over like nothing was going on whatsoever. Once it had jumped up against Stone's chest to sniff him and make sure that he actually was the Chow Boy and not some imposter, the animal dropped back down on all fours and turned with a happy tongue-hanging look toward the Indians. Excaliber barked twice, but this time in more friendly fashion as if to say, hey who the hell are you guys? Any friend of Chow Boy's is a pal of mine!

But the braves' demeanor hardly changed; their eyes still wide, they were still backing away, not really wanting to get too close. Something was getting to them. Stone wished he'd paid more attention to his "Primitive gods" lecture in anthropology back in college. Dogs, dogs—what the hell did they represent to a bunch of lost Indians?

"You—you come with us," the brave addressed Stone, but much more haltingly now, unsure of himself. "Me, Cracking Elk, son of Buffalo Breaker. Take you to chief. He must decide." The brave glanced over at the dog as flickers of fear raced across his features like a swarm of bugs. "You can control dog from biting?" Cracking Elk asked with a little contemptuous grin as if he really didn't care about it much one way or another.

"Sure," Stone lied, knowing that though the pit bull had certainly helped him on numerous occasions when the shit had hit the fan, making it attack or hold back was a different matter. "Yeah, he'll do pretty much what I say, right, pal," Stone said, leaning over to scratch the animal behind the ears. Only problem was he had forgotten for a moment that his right leg was cracked like a child's old toy, and as he shifted his weight onto the wounded leg, a bolt of pain shot up through his nervous system and he tumbled to the ground, like a scarecrow fallen from its perch, and crashed straight down onto the sand.

The only good thing about the stone-faced stoicism of Indians Stone decided at that moment was that though they didn't act too friendly, they also didn't laugh at the asshole sprawled below them on the ground. Stone didn't like this being wounded business, it made him feel much too vulnerable.

"Here," Cracking Elk said without expression, handing him a stick to use as a crutch. The one Stone had used before no doubtless had been ground into toothpicks floating twenty miles downriver.

"Thanks," Stone said, trying to look into the brave's eyes with an offer of friendship. But the chief's son would have none of that, and he looked away coldly. Stone knew he had no choice but to go with them. If he'd had his firearms it would have been different story. But without the slightest weapon, even with the dog on his side, he would be slaughtered by this crew. He'd just have to play it by ear and try to find out fast why the red men feared Excaliber so.

The Indians led him off into the woods that ran alongside the river. Here the solid land between riverbank and the towering mountains that followed along was nearly half a mile, so there was plenty of forest and wildlife, which Stone could hear scampering around in the distance. Cracking Elk and two others led and the rest followed behind Stone, escorting him along like a prisoner of war. They kept a wary eye on him, hands resting on their stabbers, as if Stone was about to make a running one-legged dash off into the shrubbery. As he stumbled along trying to get used to walking with just one appendage, Stone got the chance to look closer at their painted bodies. They were a strange breed. The things they had adorned themselves with were a bizarre mix of modern and ancient. Beads and wolf teeth were worn around necks but on some feet Stone saw beat-up old tennis sneakers. Several of the braves wore leather thongs around their waists to hold up their buffalo or buckskin pants, but again Stone noticed that two of them had mass-produced belts, one a black patent leather number, the other some sort of silvery rippling thing like a disco belt. The contrast of different accessories was quite striking. But Stone knew better than to criticize a murderous band of Indians' dress habits.

They led him on twisting, hardly noticeable paths through the thick woods. The sky had lightened from very dark to a slate gray, the rain at last diminishing to just a thin spray. It was hard to see his way and Stone kept nearly falling, having to wobble along on one leg, and, to make matters worse, the pit bull kept winding back and forth all around him so that the damned creature kept tripping him up. Excaliber, assuming the Indians were friends, felt playful and kept looking up at Stone as if to say, "Well, aren't we all having a good time?" The Indians stayed clear of the pit bull, which seemed to hurt the animal's feelings. Whenever it drew close to one of them in playful jumps, they would back off. Again Stone saw that same peculiar and deep fear in every man's eyes.

It took about fifteen minutes to reach the camp, though they would have gotten there much faster if Stone hadn't been limping along like a wounded soldier returning from the front. Then suddenly they came through a grove of firs and there it was, the strangest little encampment Stone had ever seen. There were about twenty completely round structures perhaps ten feet high, shaped somewhat like igloos only they were all made of tires. Car tires, truck tires—you name it, you could find it in the wall of somebody's home. When he was on better terms with this crew, Stone vowed, he'd ask them just where they bought their construction materials.

But he had to wonder if he'd ever get to pose the question, as they approached the edge of the Indian village, set off with a small, completely encircling fence made of branches piled atop one another. For rising above the open space in the branch barricade were heads dangling from ropes tied to a long pole stretched across the opening. There were five buffalo skulls, and two human. The flesh of the buffalo skulls had long ago disappeared so they were basically slabs of bone that looked as if they'd had little patches of fur glued not very symmetrically over their surfaces. The human heads looked as if they'd been stripped from their bodies within weeks, months at most. The flesh had hardened, pulled in, so they still looked like human faces carved out of leather. Eyes had turned into horrid black eggs, beef jerky lips shriveled up into little mouth-cracking grins as if it was all a big joke. Stone swore he saw the eyes of one moving to keep a scope on him. He gulped hard and tore his own eyes away, vowing not to look at the damned things ever again.

As they walked beneath the head greeting committee the Indians around the camp saw that their returning warriors had brought back some strange cargo. Evidently they didn't get a hell of a lot of visitors in these parts, for every man, woman, and child in the village dropped whatever they were doing, rose, and headed quickly over to see what God had wrought. Their faces didn't look too inviting; maybe they were trying to visualize how Stone's head would look up there as an addition to their small but highly regarded skull welcoming sign.

But when they caught sight of the dog trotting along half hidden behind Stone's legs, the Indians' faces took on a different look—one of stark terror. They backed off, talking wildly to one another in dialect that was incomprehensible to

Stone, not that he was an expert in Indian lingo. Still this stuff sounded like it might be spoken on Uranus. Whatever power the mutt had over the sons of bitches Martin Stone would play to the hilt. The ninety-pound ball of ass-kicking pit bull was his only chance in this rapidly deteriorating scene. But the question still was why the hell did they react to the dog as they did? Stone looked down for a second at the loping animal and was suddenly thankful he had treated the canine to a stomach-filling load of Dog Gourmet Crackers that he had found weeks before. He hoped the beast remembered.

Suddenly Stone was pushed hard by the shoulder and he nearly fell forward, barely managing to stop himself with the stick before he toppled to the ground. He raised his eyes and saw sitting ten feet in front of him, on a throne made from a huge red leather reclining seat, one of the biggest and ugliest men he had ever seen. The man was a giant, obviously the chief. What made it obvious was his feather headdress made of countless different colored feathers that trailed down his back all the way to the ground.

The man's body was huge, spilling out over both sides of the seat, which was itself quite large, one of those pre-Collapse era couches that could pull out into a bed. His huge stomach poked out of his center like a beer barrel ready to explode. He must have weighed five-hundred pounds if he weighed an ounce. Yet it was the face that caught Stone's attention. It was ugly, hideously ugly. One eye had been ripped out or destroyed by disease many years before. The chief had replaced it with a black stone just about the size and general shape of an eye, fitted into the optic opening. Looking at it was like staring into the very blackness of space, into a vacuum. The whole right side of his face was paralyzed into a stretched-out grimace, probably the result of a stroke, Stone thought, as he had seen such paralysis before. It made the chief look as if one side of his face was trying to scream, trying to let out a howl of mad horror, while the other side was completely normal, and it stared at Stone with a cold hatred.

"Down, white bastard," a voice screamed out behind him. "Bow to Chief Buffalo Breaker." A hand pushed at Stone's back again, hard. This time he couldn't stop his fall in time and slammed down onto the ground, flat on his face. He heard a sharp growl behind him and barely had time to push himself up with his hands, screaming at Excaliber to stop. The dog didn't take kindly to Stone being slammed around. The pit bull had gone into its preattack crouch, and the brave who had pushed Stone was backing off step by slow step, his eyes big as onions, as he moved. Stone knew that they'd both be dead meat if the dog snapped even one mouthful of flesh from the bastard. He reached over and grabbed the bull terrier, pulling hard at the dog's ear, catching him totally off balance for a moment. The animal tumbled over onto its side, and with a pissed-off look, cooled off. The pit bull sat back on its haunches but glanced around at the brave, who had joined the crowd of about a hundred or so Indians who now stood in a full circle around the captive and their chief.

"Who are you?" the chief asked, raising a huge staff that had once been a mop handle—only now attached to the steel clamp that had held the string mop was a long red fox tail, all that was left of the creature that had once flashed it proudly. These guys had a strange sense of decoration.

"I'm Stone," he answered, raising himself up only enough to address the fellow, but not so much as to start some big brouhaha again over showing the proper respect. "Who are you?"

"Chief Buffalo Breaker. Run whole river. Our river, Wasatawa River—our world. You trespasser." Then the chief seemed to hesitate as he looked at the dog. He seemed to become unsure just how to proceed, and studied the creature closely. Excaliber stared straight back at him with its own unflinching orbs. At last, as if the animal's will was stronger than the tub of lard squashing down into his recliner so that its four legs dug nearly six inches into the dirt, the chief looked away.

He turned back to Stone and tried to ask casually, though his voice seemed to catch in his throat, "That your dog?"

"Like I said to one of your associates," Stone said, looking up from the dirt, where he had raised himself to a half sitting position that no one seemed to think overly insulting to officialdom, "he's his own damned dog—we're sort of traveling companions, business associates or something."

The chief grunted and then grew silent again as Stone quickly looked at the crazy artwork decorating the poles staked into the ground behind the reclining chair. There were perhaps two dozen of the totem poles spread out in a semicircle behind the big man, each ten-foot pole with heads of beasts and mythical symbols carved into it. Stone swept his glance around quickly and saw why the Indians had acted as if the dog was some great honcho. Looking up he saw the animal's face, sculpted from river mud, high atop two of the poles in the dead center of the magical circle. It didn't look exactly like Excaliber but it did have the same sort of elongated face, the same almost oriental-looking eyes. Of course these particular clay dogs did have wings and talons, but if the Indians wanted, Stone would be glad to glue some on the pit bull. Obviously they worshipped some damn creature from their distant past who just happened to look like Excaliber's great-great-grandfather, give or take a few hundred generations. There was gold in that there fur.

"But dog obeys you?" the chief asked again, coughing as if it was no big deal but he just happened to be curious about it.

"Damned right he does," Stone lied. "Follows my every command, in a snap. Why, I could make him run, jump or even fly if I had a mind to," Stone said, looking hard at the chief. The fat man looked momentarily stunned by that bit of information and the lard-covered adam's apple bobbed up and down like an elevator unsure of what floor to stop on. The chief lifted his foxtail staff and banged it twice and a whole bevy of feather-headed, copper-skinned, warpainted braves flew out of the woodwork, instantly surrounding Breaking Buffalo. Stone could hear all kinds of talking and whispering, then what sounded like an argument between some of the indians. Their eyes kept turning to look at the dog, then up at the sacred sculptures of the tribe's main god. They just didn't seem able to quite believe it. But they had to.

After about five minutes the crowd cleared away again. The chief pulled a lever on the side of the huge red leather chair and the whole seat slid forward, almost depositing the load of humanity onto the ground. But Breaking Buffalo held on to the armrests on each side of him and after everything settled down, now lying almost in a reclining position, his head back on a beaver pelt pillow, the chief spoke up.

"Stone Man, you stay. Take dog and go with braves. They show you where. I talk to *all* the gods. I talk to Myhwhanka, the Hawk Dog. He will decide whether you live or die."

"Sounds good," Stone said as two of the braves came over, helped him to his feet, and started leading him off. "I'll be looking forward to talking with you again." And the thought flashed through his mind as mad thoughts do when one is completely and deliriously desperate that perhaps he could somehow sneak up at night and tie Excaliber to one of the poles with some leather thongs or something. At least get a little inside help on the chief's tribal god powwow.

## CHAPTER

# Seven

LIVING in a house made of tires was not exactly Stone's idea of Lifestyles of the Rich and Famous. He'd much rather that they had chained him outside or something. Not that it wasn't comfortable inside the twenty-foot-round structure in which everything was made of tires—walls, chairs, tables. . . . The problem was the smell. The damn tires still smelled like the rubber they were made of even though most of them seemed years old. Excaliber didn't seem to appreciate the odor as he kept running up to the wall, to the narrow openings between the piled-up dough-nuts, trying to suck in some fresh air. Stone made a quick reconnoiter of the whole structure, even managing to climb up to the ceiling by using the air vents as footholds. But though he covered just about every square inch of the place he couldn't find any opening that anything bigger than a softball could squeeze through. And though the tires looked as if they were just piled on top of one another, so he should be able to knock the top ones off, he couldn't. Either the damn things had been glued together with some sort of resin or they were attached by some hidden method that Stone couldn't see from the inside. Either way, he appeared to be here for the duration.

After about ten minutes he heard some sounds at the door, which was two immense truck tires that could be rolled over the opening. Two braves standing guard outside the structure rolled them away, and one of the tribe came walking in searching around first for Stone, then the dog with his eyes. If the chief looked strange this fellow looked positively alarming. His entire face was painted blue, his lips and nose red, his arms purple. He looked at a glance like three bizarre races, all from different planets, that had been stapled to-gether. The Indian wore all kinds of skins, snakes, teeth, and god knew what all that covered his entire body and hung almost to the floor, giving off a stench of their own. Around the Indian's neck was an immense necklace, a collection of flattened tin cans—Budweiser, Miller, Coke—names, colors that brought back a sudden storm of memories from the old days before the barbarians had taken over.

The Indian shook a long rattlelike device in his right hand, a contraption made out of old pipes and plumbing valves into which ball bearings had been sealed so it made a clang-ing metallic sound. With his left hand he sprinkled a green-ish liquid, throwing out drops all over the place like the pope entering a holy city to consecrate the grounds. The brave

clearly was trying to create some magical protection from
the stranger—and the demon dog. The medicine man, Stone
decided, as the man made chanting noises that passed for
singing and did his spray-and-rattle thing with great gusto.
The two braves at the entrance looked for a few seconds,
then shuddered as if they didn't like to look too closely at
magic lest they get their own asses burned, and pushed the
six-foot-high tractor tires back into place.

The medicine man danced right around the entire structure
keeping a wary eye on the pit bull, which merely lifted its
head slightly from an airhole where it had been trying to get
a half doze and escape from the nightmare of the place.
Stone watched in amazement, sitting back on his ass, his
ripped leg stretched out in front of him. The bastard was a
real medicine man, like the fucking late movies on TV. In
spite of his use of modern artifacts Stone had to admit he
looked like the real thing, gave a good show.

But the moment the tires were rolled back into place so
they were sealed up again, Stone wondered for the tenth
time in as many minutes just what the hell was going on. For
this particular shaman suddenly rushed over to him and
hissed out in perfect English, "Thank God I can dispense
with all this fucking Indian mumbo jumbo." He threw the
rattle and the vial of putrefying frog blood down on the dirt
floor.

"What the hell?" Stone half stuttered, his mouth dropping
open in disbelief at the words and the perfect diction of the
magic man.

"Nanhanke—numero uno witch doctor," the blue-faced
brave said, holding out a hand. "Also known as Flashing
Hand aka John Linderstein."

"What the—" Stone could only reiterate as he limply took
the offered hand, which pumped his with enthusiasm.

"You don't know how glad I am to talk to someone from
the outside. I've been stuck here for three years, three years.
But we'll talk later, man. Your leg—it's broken." He started
to lean down as if to grab hold of it, but Stone held up his
hand. The man spoke so fast and moved with such frenetic

energy that Stone wondered if he was partaking of some medicine-man herbs on the side. Of course, having his face painted blue didn't help to engender trust in Stone's guts either.

"Whoa, slow down pardner. I like to know who I let touch my leg, you know what I mean? Who are you? Who are these Indians? What the hell is going on here?" Stone asked, his voice rising excitedly so he even set Excaliber to growling and letting out with a few barks just to let the world know he was included in the complaint.

"Shhhh," the witch man said, putting his fingers to his purple lips. "Can't let them hear us." He turned and glanced at the door, picked up the rattle and shook it, screaming out Indian chants as he danced around the place a few times. Stopping suddenly he ran silently over to the front two tires and looked through quickly. Seeing that the two guards didn't give a flying fuck about what was going inside, in fact would just as soon have nothing to do with the practices of witchery, the Indian turned and walked with a half smile back to Stone, who still didn't trust the maniac worth a damn.

"There, now we're alone," he said as his face lit up with a smile that seemed to give the man a much better feeling than it gave Martin Stone. It wasn't that Stone wasn't more than ready to find anyone in this damn place who would help him, it was just that staring into a smiling mouth filled with filed-down teeth, with purple lips around it was not doing wonders for the doctor-patient relationship.

"Listen pal," Stone said, "just tell me what the hell's going on around here. You want to help me, *that* will help me. First, who the hell are you bastards?"

"We're the Atsana—the Hidden Ones or Those Who Live from the River, depending on how you translate from the Indian. The tribe came here many years ago, attracted by the hidden valleys—for as you've probably already discovered it's virtually impossible to get in and out by mountains, only water. And the river is over three hundred miles long, every bit of it covered with rapids and more rapids. It's probably one of the most hidden areas in the entire country. Anyway when the tribe learned of the total collapse of the American government, of the anarchy and warlords that descended on the outside world, they cut off what little communication they had with it five years ago. All the canoes were burned, any sort of communication with the outside totally severed. So the Atsana stayed on, living off what wildlife there is on the two-mile strip of shoreline here, and of course off what the river brings on her murderous waves, which is bountiful."

He held up one of the can tops from around his neck. "Got these fresh—can you believe it?—four crates of beer, just floating along. We get everything from the river. Floods upstream have brought a treasure trove of materials over the years. Chairs, tables, TV sets—not that we can do anything with them. Boxes filled with all kinds of junk, bodies, clothes, plywood. And one day, about two years ago, a flood of tires. The whole village was out there plucking tires out of the river for three days. As you can see we built a whole village with the booty. Strong, aren't they?" He pounded his fist against one of the walls with pride.

"I see," Stone said, starting to get at least a glimmering of the picture. "And you?" he asked, for the blue-faced son of a bitch didn't fit even into the madness of the junk-collecting tribe.

"I . . . I am half indian," the magic man said, "born into a blackfoot tribe about three hundred miles from here. I was lucky—or unlucky, depending on how you look at it. When I was fourteen the federal government decided to throw a few bucks the Indians' way and they set up this super accelerated tutorial program to help get some of the braves of my tribe into college, so we could return later and help our own. Good idea. It lasted of course only about six years, actually helped maybe three of us before the politicians decided to put the money into some new weapons system or something. But in that time I was able to get into college and then with a special scholarship into medical school." Stone looked at the graffiti-covered witch man with incredulity.

"That's right, Stone—I'm a doctor. A real doctor. All this"—he waved the rattle for a second—"is bull. It's what *they* want to see, and I know how to give it to them. After medical school I *did* return to my own tribal reservation determined to set up a practice and help my people get real medical treatment for the first time in their lives. Only thing was, I was on my way home when a nuke just happened to come down about twenty miles from the reservation. By the time I arrived there wasn't a hell of a lot left to treat. They were already all dead or dying from radiation poisoning. Teeth coming out like spilled marbles, hair—the strength of an Indian—falling out like scythed hay. Bald, bleeding Indians. Quite a sight to see. So when the last one croaked—a baby, only three, who fell apart in my hands, its destroyed cells actually turning to an ooze that dripped down and burned my arms. . . . But anyway, when it died there was no reason to stay anymore. And having not a hell of a lot to live for I just sort of walked around in a daze for nearly a week, not eating or sleeping or anything. It was like I had gone over the edge of madness. When I came to the river about a hundred miles upstream I dove in. I wanted to die but, god knows how, somehow I became entangled in a tree. I fell in and out of consciousness for what seemed like months. When I came to, I was here. And being an Indian, they let me live unlike the others they've fished out. And being the smart cookie that I am, and having medical skills, I soon saw that if I played the whole thing right I could become a real power in the village. And though my people were dead, at least I could be aiding my race, my blood."

The man took a deep breath and Stone realized that he had told his entire life history in one great blast of air and words. The fellow was definitely on something.

"And the dog?" Stone asked, pointing over at Excaliber, who didn't seem interested in the witch man's rap and had turned completely over in the other direction, his nose buried as deeply as possible into the narrow opening between

two tires as he sucked in the outside air. He seemed to hate
the rubbery scent even more than Stone. But then his nostrils
were ten thousand times more sensitive.

"Your mutt there—a pit bull if I remember my interspe-
cies anatomy, happens to resemble Myhwhanka, the Hawk
Dog, the most powerful of the tribe's gods. The Hawk Dog
runs the whole fucking show. They're scared shit of your
animal. They're not really sure what to do about it. I don't
think the chief really believes it is Myhwhanka, but on the
off chance that it is, he has to be extremely careful. For the
Hawk Dog is the bringer of death, total destruction, when he
bares his fangs. I really don't know what's going to happen
to you, Stone, I swear. I'll do what I can, but it's not much.
Though I'm a medicine man I'm just one of five here, and
the lowest on the totem pole so to speak. They let me perform certain ceremonial functions and help a few kids who
get sick, but I can't do much. The reason they sent me in
here to investigate the supernatural potential of the situation
is because it was beneath the rest of the witch boys' stations
to come. They got a strong union. Also I'm the most expen-
dable in case something goes wrong." The purple lips
stopped moving for the first time in a minute and smiled,
again showing those filed-down vampirelike stumps that
Stone had a hard time looking at.

"Just one more question," Stone said, sitting up and rubbing his leg, which had begun throbbing painfully, sending
rivers of fire up and down his nervous system. "Why the hell
should *you* help me, pal? You're one of them, I'm a paleface. What's in it for you?"

"Believe it or not I still try to follow the Hippocratic Oath
—you know, that corny old thing about helping others.
Once I get everyone out of whatever rubber teepee I've been
called to I always ask to be left alone with the patient. Then
after I do my rattle bull I go to this." He pulled a black
leather medical satchel from beneath his rotting fur robes
and threw it to the ground next to Stone's leg. "This too
came floating down one day. I managed to barter it away
from the finder with some rather potent hallucinogenic

mushrooms I find very useful as exchange around here, since these fellows love to commune with the gods. Anyway why the hell, *shouldn't* I help you?" he asked. "Whether I look like a psychotic savage to you is irrelevant. I assure you, Stone, I do know what I'm doing. Top of my class— Boston Med."

He took a glistening scalpel from the bag and leaned down again toward Stone's leg. Excaliber looked over suddenly, sensing the drawing of a cutting implement. The dog started to rise until Stone motioned it down.

"Relax, dog, he's a vet." The animal closed its eyes and harrumphed disgustedly, snorting air out through its nose like a whale clearing its breathing tubes. "All right, doc . . ." Stone faltered on the words, again looking into that nightmarish face. But he went with his instincts. "Do your thing, doc . . . whatever that is," Stone said, lying back and gritting his teeth.

The witch man lifted the rattle and shook it loudly at the door, letting loose with a few war cries just so it didn't get too quiet inside. "Love this job," he said, as he sliced the blood-soaked pants all around the fractured leg so he could get a better look.

"But listen, Stone, there is a price for my medical talents: tell me what the hell's going on out there. A number of times I've thought about leaving. It's, uh, interesting here but not exactly the peak of intellectual or social stimulation." He cut the pants open and peeled back both already hardening pieces of material to see just what the avalanche had wrought on breakable flesh.

"Well, as far as I've seen," Stone replied, resting his arms back behind his head against one of the tires, "you're just as smart to stay here until hell freezes over. It's bad out there. It's horrible. A place that should only exist in nightmares and grade C horror movies. If I were you I'd stay put. You got a good job, security. Probably grow old and become top witch man, maybe even run the show."

"That's about what I figured," Nanhanke said as he stood back from his close inspection of the wound. "You could see

from a lot of the stuff that floated downriver—especially the
bodies—that the world had taken a decided turn for the
worse in the last few years. Just wanted to confirm it, I
guess."

"Well, consider it confirmed," Stone said. "As bad as you
visualize it, it's worse."

"All right, Stone, I've got good news and bad news," the
medicine man said, shaking the rattle about five times and
then dropping it down. "The good news is that your leg is
healing nicely."

"And the bad?" Stone asked, fearing the worst.

"The bad is that it's healing improperly, at an angle. Once
the bone re-fuses with itself you'll walk with a pronounced
limp, maybe won't even be able to run or anything. Not
exactly a survival trait in the outside, I would imagine."

"So what's the treatment?" Stone asked nervously, knowing that whatever it was, it was going to hurt like hell.

"There's only one thing I can do: try to force the damned
thing back into a straight alignment. But it's already started
healing . . . so . . . so"

"So, spit it out man. Christ, your bedside manners leave
something to be desired."

"So I'm going to have to rebreak it, maybe slam the living
shit out of it to get the bone back into place."

"You're kidding," Stone whispered, his face growing
white.

"No joke about it, gringo," Nanhanke said with a grin,
trying but failing to lighten the tense mood. "Either I do my
best or it's cripple time for the Stone man."

"Go ahead then," Stone said, getting a sinking and dark
feeling in his guts. He wasn't afraid of dying, but there was
something about being torn to pieces bit by broken bit that
he wasn't looking forward to at all.

"Better warn your dog there to cool it if you start screaming or something. Because I can promise you only one thing
—it will hurt."

"Excaliber," Stone yelled, cupping one hand over his
mouth. "Shut up!" He figured if he prewarned the dog it

would listen. But the canine was already fast asleep and in much too pleasant a dream to pay Stone's admonitions from the real world the slightest heed.

"Go ahead man, do your fucking thing," Stone said, gritting his teeth.

The Indian moved fast as if he wanted to get it over with quickly. He grabbed hold of the inner rim of a tire about six feet up and getting a good grip, suddenly jumped up in the air and came down with both feet right on the broken bone. Stone let out a scream that surprised even him. And Nanhanke rattled madly at the door while he let his patient settle down. Once Stone's mouthings had dropped to dull hisses of torture, the witch man got down on his knees and examined the wound.

"Good, good, I did it—or very close. Now we'll just—" He reached out without giving Stone any warning, and grabbing at the leg with both hands slammed the two pieces against one another with all the strength of his 230-pound, well-muscled body. He was, after all, an Indian. This time Stone actually managed to keep the scream to a long whistling trainlike sound that went on for a full minute. For though it hurt like a bitch, he could suddenly sense that the bone *did* fit properly now. It was as if his whole leg suddenly felt straight, as it should be.

"I think you . . . you actually fixed it," Stone said, reaching down to touch the wounded area.

"Uh-uh," Nanhanke said, slapping down at Stone's hands. "Don't touchee now," he mocked him as if addressing a child. "Infection, that's going to be your biggest worry now. I'll squirt some of this Indian goo on. It really works, has antibiotic properties." He inundated the still-oozing split skin that stretched half way around the leg with a greenish substance that felt both cool and instantly soothing on Stone's torn flesh. "And then we'll just throw some white man's bandages on here." He wrapped some sterile gauze around the wound and tied it all down with thin threads of buffalo intestine.

"Jesus Christ," Stone blurted out in sheer amazement as the witch doctor stood back and surveyed his work.

"No—Nanhanke," the medicine man chuckled, his broken teeth reflecting the light that flowed in from outside. "Wish I had a business card to give you." He patted at his animal hides and fox-jaw necklaces as if he might have somehow misplaced one somewhere inside. "Well anyway, that's all I can do. God help you, Stone, Indian and gringo gods alike. It's out of my hands now. Just keep in close proximity to your bird dog there, he's your ace in the hole."

"Thanks, Dr. Linderstein," Stone said half mockingly, addressing the man with his other alias. "I won't forget it."

"Don't mention, don't mention," Nanhanke said, starting toward the door. He began waving his rattle again, dancing up and down as he chanted deep guttural sounds like a dying man clearing his throat. He screamed at the tires and the braves quickly pulled them back, letting him exit. They loaded in some food—two big bowls, each holding a good gallon of steaming stuff. Since the chief felt he had to be hospitable to the possible dog god, they were both given a stew of the tenderest venison.

Excaliber's eyes lifted from out of deep sleep at the scents suddenly wafting over his nose, which were even stronger than the wretched rubbery smell. He was at his bowl and slobbering up a virtual eruption of the steaming food before Stone had a chance to lift his fork. Yea, though we walketh into the shadow of the Valley of Death—let's eat first.

# Eight

STONE had to admit that the Atsana treated him pretty well—for a man who was most likely headed for the grave, that is. For he had no illusions about the future of things. They were still unsure of just what the hell to do with him and his crazy dog and held endless meetings on the subject. But at least they treated him as if they were following the Geneva convention on POW treatment—plenty of food, care for his wound, and shelter. Only problem was he couldn't go anywhere, just stayed locked inside the tire prison with shifts of braves waiting out front in case he got any funny gringo ideas.

But at least he could see out the slits and cracks between the tires. From the moment he awoke the next morning, after a heaping breakfast of corn gruel and nuts, he spent the rest of the morning and afternoon glued to the openings in the igloo of black rubber trying to find out everything he could about the Indian village, its beliefs, its people. Any information he could pick up might mean the difference between life and death. Stone remembered being out in the mountains with his father, the major. He was only six and they were coming down a mountain path when Clayton Stone stopped in his tracks and put his hand on his son's shoulder to stop him, putting his fingers to his lips at the same time. He pointed down at some tracks in the inch or so of freshly fallen snow.

"Mountain cat, Martin, see?" The boy looked down.

Stone remembered being both very cold, his breath falling
from his mouth like liquid oxygen from the tail of a rocket,
and at the same time very excited. A mountain lion. He had
never seen one. "It's the little things that tell you everything
son, see." He traced the outline of the track with his finger.
"We know by the size and shape of the foot what it is, and
by the fact that the edges are still almost straight, not
rounded off by the wind, that he's probably within a hundred
yards of us. It's the little things around you that reveal
everything." And though Stone could hardly believe that
even his father could predict such things, lo and behold they
moved on slow and quiet as possible and within seventy-five
yards came to a good-sized cat behind a bush ripping away
at a cottontail. The lion looked at them, they looked at the
lion, and young Martin's heart sped up to the beat of a drum
machine. But it was the lion who broke and ran first. The
little things. They revealed all. So Stone set to find those
little things in every action, every movement he could make
out through the slits and cracks of the tire palace.

Excaliber as well seemed to have found ways to occupy
himself. The dog had discovered that it could use the spaces
between the tires to sort of half climb/half hang off the wall.
And by taking a good running jump the animal was actually
able to scamper right up the side of one of the walls nearly to
the ceiling where, after a few frantic seconds of trying to get
a hold on anything at all, it would fall back to the earth
below with a thud. But the dog was so tough that it wasn't
fazed. And each time, the canine would rise up again,
bouncing right off the earthen floor like a ball, get a good
running jump, and try again. No matter how many falls it
only seemed to drive the terrier to greater efforts. It virtually
flew up along the walls and ceiling like some sort of misfit
that had neither the physiology nor the muscular abilities to
climb.

Meanwhile, Stone was fascinated by what he observed
outside. It was like looking back onto a primitive world,
almost prehistoric. Men had doubtless lived like this ten
thousand years ago. Carrying water in gourds from the river,

living off the fish pulled from the roaring waters with crude
nets they had set out. Women on their knees wearing thick
buffalo and buckskin outfits grinding corn kernels that had
been stored from the summer before, into paste for breads
and crackers. Young braves running around half naked as
they played at spearing one another with branches, shooting
each other with imaginary bows and arrows, each one taking
turns to kill and then be killed. Everywhere there was a
myriad of activity and over the hours Stone counted at least
a hundred people as he tried to keep mental track of those
who went by.

After a while in fact, he came to recognize and name—at
least in his own mind—those he was observing. There was
the Old Lady with a Face Like Leather Who Could Carry a
Thousand Pounds. She would go up and down the hill on
one side of Stone's rubber home with a look of supreme
patience on her copper red face filled with cracks and rivu-
lets that life had chiseled across her features. Down the hill
to the river, filling four huge gourds with water and then
carrying them back up balancing them on a long pole that
she carried over her shoulders. Just by the way the pole bent
Stone knew that the weight was 150, possibly 200 pounds,
far more than the ancient squaw's weight. When people
didn't know they "couldn't" do something, they seemed to
have the remarkable ability to do it.

Then there was the Hunter Who Liked to Brag for Hours.
Stone sort of liked the guy. A huge brave, garbed in a bizarre sort of costume created of equal parts of bear pelt and
plastic spandex ribbing in the arms and waist, with football
shoulder protectors sewn in with leather thongs around the
shoulders. Then a baseball cap with NY METS on it, feathers
stuck in top through the green sunglass visor that had been
built into the brim for watching games. The combination of
styles gave the yellow striped face a look of something the
avant garde fashion designers of Soho and Paris were playing with before there were no more clothes to design and no
more stores to sell them in. Still the guy could doubtless
have made quite a hit back in the right circles. But he

seemed to be doing pretty good right here. The Indian had
bagged a moth-bitten mountain goat and had dragged it
back, depositing it on the ground where he proceeded to
spend hours bragging to whoever he could get to stop how
big the thing was.

Though the Indians seemed to take pride in how they
looked, many of them had physical infirmities and deformi-
ties. Most had lost their teeth and had mouths of wooden
teeth that kept coming out. Others were missing arms,
hands, a leg here and there. And as always, as Stone had
seen throughout his travels, radiation burns and the resultant
symptoms and diseases caused by it. Some of the children
were the worst. Their parents would have been exposed to
high levels of radioactivity out here. Stone had seen two
H-craters within a hundred miles of the place. And it was
their children who had paid the price for those who lived to
breed, for many were deformed, some quite horribly. Arms
twisted at odd chicken-wing like angles, faces missing chins
or ears, lips where noses should have been, three eyes. Even
a pair of completely legless boys. And yet he had to hand it
to all of them, to the sheer tenacity of the Atsana spirit. For
the ugly bastards played and laughed and ran with the others
like the healthiest of children. Even the legless ones were
carried, the eyeless ones were led. All were allowed to join
in, all screamed out in wild childish laughter.

Late that afternoon, after he had had a huge bowl of corn
soup and slabs of venison, and he and the dog were just
stretching out for a little post-imbibing siesta, the pseudo
medicine man showed up, with his usual rattling and snake
dancing, to check on his patient. After the guards had rolled
the two huge tractor tires back in front of the entrance he
took off his headdress, an upside down boot with a Dolly
Parton wig hanging down over it.

"Damn, this thing is heavy—you'd be amazed," Nanhanke said, and as always Stone could hardly believe the
almost New York accent that emerged from the purple lips.

"I can imagine," Stone said, sitting up from his prone
position.

"How's the leg?" the Indian asked as he walked over, tucking his rattle in his belt and leaning his huge mop-handled scepter against the tire wall.

"Not as bad as it was," Stone answered, looking down at the appendage. "I don't know if it's healing, but it sure as hell doesn't hurt as much as it did before you dropkicked it for a field goal."

"Good, good," the medicine man exclaimed, bending down and pulling back the split sides of the pants leg. "Less pain is a sign that the bones are fusing more properly together. The body doesn't like things not to fit right, so it lets you know. Pain is the language that it speaks." He got down on the earth floor on his hands and knees and sighted up along the leg like sighting down a pool cue to see if it was straight before heading for the table.

"Looking good, looking real good," the witch man said, rising up again. "Couldn't have done better if I was back in Union General and had a whole team of surgeons, an operating room, and malpractice insurance and everything. I think the damn thing is going to heal almost perfectly. You're incredibly lucky, Stone. You came millimeters from being a cripple for the rest of your life."

"Well, I've already got mental problems," Stone smirked, "might as well have the body to go along with it." He looked hard at the Atsana. "Tell me, how's it going out there? I mean as far as I'm concerned. I can see they've been pow-wowing all day."

"Don't know, man," Nanhanke replied, leaning up against the tires and looking out as if trying to see what Stone had been gazing at. "The chief's so uptight on this one that he won't let any but his top two men in on the actual decision making. Me and the other four witch doctors ain't even allowed in on the negotiations. I think the truth is"—he paused—"he's scared shit of that damned dog and he don't want no one to know it except his most trusted pals. Don't want to look bad to the rest of the tribe. That dog plays an incredible role in the religious and historical background of the tribe. It's sort of like Jesus Christ, George Washington,

and Thomas Edison all rolled up into one." The medicine
man looked over at the dog, who was half asleep with one
eye open just a crack looking straight back at the Indian. He
swore it could see right into his brain. "And sometimes I
wonder myself."

"Oh, he's just a damned dog, and not a very good one at
that," Stone said, annoyed at the glorification of the overeat-
ing, overburping, and overfarting canine. He paused, and
looked hard again at the witch doctor. "Listen, what about
your helping me to escape, just even—"

"Forget it, pal, no way," Nanhanke said, waving his
hands in front of him like a customer at a sales clerk who
was holding a shirt five sizes too small. "I'm glad to help
you with your leg and I sincerely wish you the best of luck.
But I'm here for the duration. I ain't going back out there.
It's only going to get worse. Here I'm a respected pillar of
the community. Got me a good job—probably work my way
to the top, Head Bullshit Talker—got me a squaw with tits
the size of watermelons, own my own all-weather teepee.
Are you kidding, I got it better now that I ever did in the old
days. No mortgage, no alimony, no way."

Stone laughed at the completion of the man's little rap.
"Okay, I think I get the message," he grinned. The guy
should have had his own ad agency. Nanhanke fitted his
headdress back on until it felt about right, the blond wig
falling down over both sides of his face. He smashed the
rattle against the tractor tires and screamed out in dialect for
the morons on the other side to open it up before he used
some magic on them, because the white man smelled and he
wanted to get the hell out of there. Nanhanke winked at
Stone just before he disappeared outside. The prisoner just
stared at the door for a long, long time.

Stone and the dog supped from more food-filled gourds
for dinner but otherwise weren't visited again. Everyone
seemed to want to stay as far away as possible from the
magic mutt, which for the moment at least was fine with
Stone. It took nearly an hour for him to fall asleep, though

the dog lapsed into blissful farting unconsciousness within seconds of eating its last bite.

Stone wasn't sure what time of the morning it was, or what the hell he was dreaming—probably something about April being sliced up by bikers. But all of a sudden he was bolt upright in the near darkness lit only by the two main campfires always kept going in the center of the camp about fifty yards off. Something was wrong. He heard a bizarre sound like someone coughing or perhaps trying to make a mating call but getting the sound stuck in their throat. Stone tried to trace the source of the sound in the flickering grayness and then heard something straight above him. He raised his eyes and saw the dog, or the lower half of it anyway, dangling straight down from the rubber-tire ceiling about ten feet above. Somehow the animal, deciding to take some four A.M. excercise, had gotten its head and right front leg and shoulder lodged into a small car tire that formed part of the roof, and couldn't for the life of itself get out. The back legs kicked madly in the air, like an angel trying to get back up into its cloud before God made bedcheck. And the sound the animal was making was pathetic—a wail filled with fear and humiliation.

"Christ, Excaliber," Stone groaned, unable to stop his mouth from stretching into a wide grin as he pushed himself up from the straw bed he had made in the corner. "You must have watched too many Three Stooges films in your childhood," Stone said smirking as he tried to figure out how the hell he could dislodge the creature. He didn't want to call the Indians in, because if they saw the mutt in such a dumb predicament all of the dog's godly and macho powers would evaporate like so many soap bubbles in the sun. No, this had to be kept in the family, to say the least.

He looked around and saw the crutch with its crook at one end for his arm to rest on. Stone grabbed the thing up and half walked, half hopped until he was standing right underneath the dog. He balanced himself on one leg until he felt good and set.

"Dog, this is going to hurt you more than me. Just grit

your incisors and we'll see what happens." There was a
whiny growl from above, the animal not very audible with
its head on the outside of the tire building. Stone pulled the
three-inch-thick branch back and whapped forward right at
the animal's flank. As he swung Stone found himself losing
his balance, and he tumbled forward along with the motion
of the blow. The branch hit the dog amidships and the animal swung up toward the rubber ceiling like a speed bag in a
gymnasium. When it bounced off the rubber and back down
again the sheer kinetic energy of the ninety pounds of dog
pulled the creature with a loud pop right out of the roof of
the vulcanized teepee, like a child popping a nipple from its
mouth. Like some previously unsighted and hopefully never
seen again meteor from the darkest nether regions of space,
the animal came hurtling down, every one of its legs spinning in the dark air at once as if flight was possible if one
just tried hard enough.

The animal came down right on Stone's shoulders just as
he was toppling forward himself, and the struggling, shout-
ing, growling pair crashed down onto the earth in a dusty
pile of flesh and fur. When it was all sorted out and every
appendage had been extricated from their pretzellike entan-
glement, Stone just sat back and tried to still his beating
heart.

"Oh dog, dog, dog, dog, dog, dog," he said over and over
again like some sort of insane mantra, as he slowly drifted
back off to sleep again seeing lines of pit bulls jumping and
biting fences.

# CHAPTER

## Nine

A BOUT three hours later, that morning, when Stone awakened and saw that it was dawn, the sky a mass of dripped ink and spilled color, he looked out the tire slot nearest his face and saw that something was up. They were building a structure of some kind in the very center of the encampment, a cleared circle about a hundred feet in diameter where much of the tribe's group interaction occurred. And it was as bizarre as anything out of *Gulliver's Travels*. As the sun hauled itself up to the tree line like an old crow that can't quite make it, Stone could make out the general shape of the structure. The shape—but not what the hell it was going to be used for. It was a rough box about eight feet long and three wide, with ropes and junk all over it. As one group of braves worked on that, testing ropes, tightening corners, another group was building a huge bonfire about twenty feet behind the structure, a mother of a fire that was already ten feet high and perhaps an equal size around. It looked like their work was only beginning as braves walked in long lines back and forth to the nearby forests, dragging more fuel.

Stone watched throughout the day as they put up poles and banners, the women getting elaborate gowns together, their hair being put up and braided by each other. Something big was in the offing, that was for damned sure. Somehow Stone had the sickening feeling that he was going to be an integral part of the festivities. They fed him breakfast and then lunch, Excaliber so chagrined by the embarrassing epi-

sode of the evening before that the dog couldn't even face
Stone but just dragged its food off to the farthest corner and
ate with its face to the wall. Then it went back to sleep, nose
pressed deep into a crevice trying to suck in fresh air. Stone
felt sorry for the stupid dog. Its macho image had been attacked and the dog had come out the loser. There's something about hanging like an ornament on a Christmas tree,
and knowing that you'd be there until hell freezes over if
you're not rescued, that does wonders for one's tough-guy
rep.

Nanhanke never showed that day, which seemed like a
bad omen to Stone. And as the sun fell blood red and
bloated from the sky like a leech that had drunk too much,
he still hadn't gotten dinner. If they weren't feeding him that
was a bad sign. It meant they didn't think it was going to
matter if he was hungry or not, and who the hell knew what
that meant. But as the twilight and then the night fell like the
shroud over a coffin, Stone grew increasingly nervous. The
dog, too, which had just been getting used to the three
squares seemed skittish, testy, and it snarled out through the
cracks at the activities going on around them.

When darkness fell the festivities began. Stone didn't
know exactly what the hell was happening, but he watched
fascinated. First the great bonfire that now topped thirty feet
high, twenty wide, was doused with some sort of flammable
liquid. Then at Chief Breaking Buffalo's command, archers
on every side of the square opened up with flaming arrows.
The pyre caught in numerous places and sprang into fire. A
great yellow funnel ripped up into the night sky like a flaming tongue trying to kiss the curvaceous clouds wiggling by
above. A second curtain of sparks and smoke and sputtering,
crackling drops of superheated resin followed behind the
flames. The wall of fire lit up the low flying clouds above
which reflected the yellows and oranges off their mile-wide
stomachs back down to the earth below, so that it almost
appeared that the sky and the earth and everything in between were on fire.

After about five minutes, once the sparks had settled

down, the braves began dancing around the fire. Stone couldn't see clearly at first, as everything was alternately in shadows and then streaks of light. But as he strained his eyes he focused in on the scene. About forty braves were running and leaping around the flames as the chief stood back near the strange wooden contraption that had been built. They wore something on their heads that made them look huge and horned, and as he squinted Stone could see bison heads —mangy brown heads as big as beach balls, with curved horns. Some of the heads looked real, others perhaps made from leather and pelts. But it was all real enough for the Indians for they got into the ritual dance with increasing enthusiasm.

Log drums pounded from the shadows around the bonfire. It sounded as if there were dozens of them, beating out an unstoppable rhythm that seemed to shake the very ground, the stars above, shake them and move them in rhythm to its syncopated tribal tempo. The buffalo-headed braves ran around the fire in all different directions smashing into one another, weaving intricate dances around one another. They pretended to gore one another and make screaming noises, throwing their heads back and baying at the flame-splattered sky as if they were in mortal agony.

After about twenty minutes of this Stone noticed other braves sneaking up on them from the shadows, fake swords and bows in their hands. They suddenly rushed forward and into the ring of "buffalo," attacking them with wild thrusts and screams of human dominance. But the buffalo fought back. Terrified at first, after a minute they seemed to gather their forces and in one great unit charged back. The humans were ripped apart and fell "dying" to the ground as the others fled back into the shadows.

Stone wished he had a video camera to record it all for posterity, if there was any. He remembered his anthro professor back at college. Son of a bitch would have thrown a shit fit to witness this. He glanced over at Excaliber but the dog couldn't care less about buffalo dances. The pit bull sniffed forlornly at the tire he had adopted as the most comfortable in the place and sniffed hard, searching for an errant scent of porridge or venison that meant dinner was coming soon. Stone turned back to his viewing slit with a grunt. The dog could use a diet anyway. Its stomach looked as if it could have been a life preserver on the *Titanic*.

Suddenly there was a great pounding on the drums. From out of the shadows walked Chiefie, all decked out in his royal duds. Even from many yards off, Stone was impressed by what he could see. The great one had on an even longer feathered headdress than he had worn the day before. This one split up into two and came down each shoulder in front of him to the ground. The feathers were luminous and shining like jewels even from fifty yards off. Beneath it he was stripped to only a loincloth made of black bear fur, as shimmering as satin. The man was immense, huge arms and chest. Buffalo Breaker came up to the circle of dancers and held his arms high to the sky. Then he lowered them and waded into the beasts, fists flying. The buffalo fell to the dirt where they lay still. It was over in seconds. All were "dead." The chief stood in front of the fire and raised his arms so Stone could see them by the flames. It was quite impressive.

But not as much as what happened next. For Stone found out what the strange box they had been building all day was for. Out of the darkness was led a shape, and as he squinted, he saw it was a cow—no, a buffalo. A real honest-to-god bison. Somehow they'd manage to scrape one up way back here in the middle of nowhere. The animal looked a bit rib-sticking and motheaten. But it was real, that was for sure. No men could saunter around, could lower their head in charge gestures like that. The buffalo was led around the fire three times as the drums pounded and the braves let out high-pitched screeches, waggling their hands over their mouths so the sound came out like a siren. The bison was led by tether over to the wooden box that had been constructed. Stone's guts relaxed just a notch as he saw that whatever horrible thing was going to happen was going to happen to a dumb beast—and not Stone and his fucking wonderdog.

Stone shifted around to get a better position against the tires, as he didn't want to miss a second. He massaged his leg, which had fallen half asleep, to make sure that the bandage around it wasn't too tight and shutting off the blood supply. Then he turned quickly back, burying his face deep in the opening. The bison was pushed, with some trouble, backwards into the pen and Stone could now see that the wooden structure had been measured exactly for the beast's specifications, for it fit the pen to a T when it was at last completely pushed inside.

Chief Buffalo Breaker raised his arms again and addressed the sky half singing, half screaming out a whole litany of Indian promises, threats, prayers. At last when all the gods had been satisfied ritual-wise, the chief walked over and stood directly in front of the bison. He stared deep into its eyes as the ropes that had been thrown around it from each side of the pen were pulled tight, effectively immobilizing it in place so that it couldn't move but a fraction of an inch in any direction. The chief seemed to be looking for something right in the center of the bison's skull, dead center between its horns, because he stared down there for about five minutes, like he was searching for gold.

Then he raised his right hand slowly, ever so slowly, like a guillotine being raised inch by agonizing inch, its slow ascent all the more terrible because of the speed at which it would descend, and the results of that descent. And when the hand was up over the chief's head as if he were reaching for the very moon, he let out a great scream that dwarfed even the mass of chanting, the beat of the log drums that echoed for miles down the canyons.

Then the hand came down and Stone saw why the chief was called He Who Breaks Buffalos' Heads. Because he did. The hand slammed down like a cleaver right between the horns or that exact spot that the chief's lifelong experience in killing the animals had shown him, the weakest spot, where the bone would give. And he was right again. This was his thirteenth buffalo, one a year for the last thirteen years. The buffalo's head was cracked clean open, right down the middle like an egg broken to throw into the omelette pan. The bone of the skull just opened up and a geyser of muck gushed up several feet into the air, blood and miscellaneous slime under the pressure of the buffalo's circulatory system.

The beast crumbled to its knees as if dropping into prayer. It had time only to let out one ghastly mooing sound that was filled with so much pain and terror that Stone felt his chest tighten up. The bison's great head seemed to shake back and forth atop its quivering body like one of those heads on a spring that Americans had once carried in the back windows of their cars. The chief suddenly reached down with both hands and dipped right into the skull pan of the bison. Digging in deep, his hands flat like two shovels, he stood up, scooping out the whole brain, trailing arteries and nerves and every goddamned thing.

The chief held the pulsing brain package up over his head as he turned and headed back to the fire about thirty feet away. The Indians let out war whoops as the drums pounded victory and the spilling of blood. With the slime dripping down over his hands the chief walked up until he was within feet of the flames and threw the bundle of tissue with all his might. It soared up, spinning and trailing a web of mucus, and then disappeared into the wall of flames in the center. There was a sudden bursting sound and then a loud pop of red flame as the tissue of the brain ignited all at once.

Suddenly there was a sound behind him and Stone turned, startled, expecting for a moment to see Excaliber entangled in something again. But it was the "door," the big tractor tires being rolled back. Two braves walked into the hut, swinging metal cans—Campbell's soup if Stone was not mistaken, though the lables were worn and discolored— filled with flaming coals. The flickering torches filled the tire teepee with shadows making their arms look ten feet long, making Stone's head appear big as a chair on the far wall. Then one of the braves, a fellow with metal can openers through each ear, his face painted red as freshly spilled blood, stared hard at Stone.

"You next," was all he said, pointing with his thumb toward the door and the fire. In his whole life Martin Stone had never hated a word as much as he did the sound of the word "next" at that moment.

## CHAPTER

# Ten

STONE walked out between the two guards as Excaliber followed sulkily along between two more. They carried long spears made of kitchen knives glued and taped around broom handles. But they didn't look terribly eager to take on the dog. Stone hobbled along on the crutch trying to look unafraid and still plenty tough, which was a little difficult as he kept almost stumbling into gopher holes in the dirt. They led him up to the chief, who was on his throne now, still wearing only the feathered hat thing and his black bear loincloth. The man's body was covered in sweat so his copper skin glowed like a freshly minted penny. The black stone in his missing eye looked as if one could fall into hell itself if one peered too long into it. So Stone focused on the other eye as the chief spoke to him.

"Good news and bad news, Stone Man," Chief Buffalo Breaker said, sitting up straight in his recliner, holding the staff as the symbol of his authority. "The good news is your dog can live. It is not the Hawk Dog, that has been decided through the flames of the bison's head. But it is a relative of the Hawk Dog and can stay here as our honored guest and be assured food and shelter as long as it desires."

"Sounds pretty good to me," Stone said, looking down at the pit bull, which glared around at the Indians as an empty stomach always made it pissed off and ready to kick ass.

"The bad news," the chief went on, rising up from his chair so his stomach popped out like a boulder about to roll down a hill, "is that *you* are not of the gods and therefore must die immediately."

"Shit," Stone spat out. "I'm not even well," he protested, raising his crutch. The other Indians started forward, thinking Stone was about to attack the head man. But it was only a dramatic gesture on his part. Stone was in no condition to go charging anyone. He let the branch fall back to the dirt as his bad leg settled its weight back on it. "At least let me heal so I can die as a complete man, not a half man."

"The rituals, the gods, the brain readings of the bison all demand that you be sacrificed as well to the Great Hawk Dog, who is hungry for human souls." Great, Stone thought, his own dog was going to live—not only that but was going to be given royal treatment in the Presidential Suite with all the fucking venison it wanted, probably even cut into little pieces—for the rest of its mangy life. While Stone was supposed to join in marshmallow roasting time, and not only that, but give *his* life to satisfy yet another hungry dog, the fucking Hawk Dog in the sky.

"I don't give a shit about your fucking buffalo brains," Stone snarled. And again the braves on each side of the chief started forward, while the medicine men waved their rattles around threateningly. "They're wrong. Brains can be wrong, right? Besides I *am* this Hawk Dog here's friend. Right, dog?" Stone yelled down at the animal, which stood about three feet away looking around for any crumbs that might have been dropped here and there. "I said, RIGHT, DOG? YOU DON'T WANT ME TO DIE. I'M YOUR MAIN MAN. RIGHT, DOG?" The animal looked up at Stone and then at the chief and let out a sudden snarl, curling its lips back on its teeth, letting its fur rise up. Stone didn't know if the animal really was sticking up for him or was pissed off at missing dinner, but it seemed to send a little scare into all of them. Stone quickly pressed the advantage.

"All right, I don't mind dying if that's the way it has to be. Who the hell am I to argue with buffalo brains. I'm sure you have some of the best brain readers around." He searched for Nanhanke among the line of witch docs behind the chief and found him after a few seconds. But the voodoo man wouldn't meet Stone's look, instead lowering his face to the ground as he shook his rattle high in the air. "But at least," Stone went on, addressing the chief, "give me the chance to fight my way out. Don't all Indians have a right to challenge, some way of seeing what the gods' true intentions are?"

"There is the right of final challenge," the chief said grudgingly. "But that is just for Indians. You are—" The dog snarled loud and this time took a step forward. The faces of all the ranks around the chief grew a touch pale at seeing their Hawk Dog's cousin or uncle or whatever the hell they figured it to be, coming straight at their number one man, saliva flowing freely from its mouth.

"Down, dog," Stone screamed, slapping his hand hard. The pit bull stopped in its tracks, lying down on all fours, but kept a demonic gaze fixed right on the chief. With the tribe all looking on, and the possibly supernatural dog baring its fangs, Chief Buffalo Breaker suddenly decided that compromise was the better part of valor and spoke up again.

"Well, I suppose you *do* have the right. We are, after all, men."

"Right, chief, exactly," Stone said with fake smile, shaking his head up and down.

"But someone must fight you. An Atsana. And you are a cripple, hardly a worthy—"

"I will fight him," a voice spoke up from the front ranks.

"Cracking Elk," the chief whispered, his voice faltering. This whole thing wasn't turning out at all the way he had set it up.

"Yes, Father," the brave said, stepping from the shadows. "I will fight him and kill him. I should have killed him back at the shore as we do all strangers." Besides being eager to kill Stone, for he genuinely hated all whites, Cracking Elk had deeper reasons to want to take him out. His father had always kept his son in his shadow. The very power and stature of the chief had made Cracking Elk almost a nonentity, nonexistent, the way a small though sturdy tree pales beside the towering oak growing next to it. The whole tribe was present on this flaming night of god power. They would see that he was strong, that he could kill even one favored by the Hawk Dog.

"Yes," Cracking Elk went on, taking off his deerskin jacket to reveal huge muscular arms. "I want very much to be the gods' warrior if this white man thinks he can challenge them." He stood back and waved his hands to both sides signaling the rest of the nearby braves to clear off and get out of the way.

"Well, I—I—" Buffalo Breaker didn't want to actually allow it to start. There was something wrong. Even though Stone had only one leg, there was just something wrong. It was his own son. But it was too late—they were all watching. The gods had been invoked, had heard the plea of the Stone man. There was no way out, even for a chief.

"Very well, the challenge may begin," Buffalo Breaker said, letting his head drop slightly, his shoulders hunch, from his usual proud bearing. For somehow, no matter what happened, the chief had been defeated in a way he couldn't even really understand.

"Now, let me get this correct," Stone said as he stripped off his own jacket with a little trouble as he had to balance on one leg. But bare-chested was apparently the way to go around here. "I win and I can leave, right? With supplies and no one playing any tricks?"

"If you win?" the chief smirked. "Yes, then you do as you wish. The gods have heard all. We do not lie about things like that."

"All right," Stone said, "what's the pitch? Choice of weapons? Sabers, dueling pistols at thirty feet?" He grinned at some of the witch doctors, trying to get on their good side. But these red- and green- and blue-painted, hay-covered, bird-nest-glued-in-their-hair witch doctors didn't quite look ready to trade a few jokes. They pointed their various rods, sticks, and carved magic totems at him and each chanted out his own little death song.

"You use what you have, Stone Man," the chief said, smiling now himself. "That *is* the challenge: that a man must survive with what he has, where he is at that moment."

"Right, I get it," Stone said, as he turned around and saw that Cracking Elk had already taken out a blade that looked a good two feet long and was flickering like a laser in the rising columns of beating fire. Stone turned fully and lifted up the green branch so he was holding it in both hands. If he had had both legs functional this would have been a snap. Among other things, he and the major had spent years in one of the back caverns of the bunker working out combat killing techniques. Not self-defense. Not something taught to grandmothers in the suburbs. But just: how to kill. The major after all had been the toughest bastard in the toughest and nastiest little war ever fought, over in Vietnam. Not to mention Korea, Cambodia, Laos . . . And the *other* guy had always died. Not his father. So Stone had paid careful attention to the lessons, even as he feuded philosophically with his old man. Stick fighting had been one of his more innate abilities. Although he wished now that he had done a little more practicing on one leg.

"All right, asshole," Stone said, trying to bait the man. He had to make the Indian come to him. There was no way in hell Stone was going to start hopping around all over the place like some kind of monoplegic rabbit. "I hear Indians' wives like to get fucked by white men," Stone laughed as he tried to balance himself so most of his weight was on his good leg. He hefted the stick between his hands, letting it slide through both palms a few times back and forth, just to get the feel of the thing and maybe to unnerve the chief's son as he saw the smooth, fast movements.

"Come on, what are you waiting for, Mr. Deer Fucker, or whatever your name is?" Stone snapped, trying desperately to get the Indian angry. But all the young and immensely strong-looking brave did was walk forward in a half crouch on his toes as stealthly as any man Stone had faced. And suddenly he was licking his lips hard. This guy looked as bad as his father. Maybe it would have been better after all to have been broiled fast in the fire and get it over with, rather than be all sushi'ed up by this overmuscled bastard.

"I'll tell you why the white man defeated the Indian when he came over here to America," Stone laughed, curling his lips back in his best imitation of Richard Widmark in *Kiss of Death*. "Because all Indians are pansies and cowards and could be beaten up by even old white women." Although absurdly stupid, the insult seemed to suddenly break through Cracking Elk's cool and he lurched forward in a sudden charge against Stone. Even though Stone had planned it, when the brave made his move Stone wasn't ready for the speed of the man. The cripple barely had time to move, let alone strike out with the staff. He was lucky to swing it up alongside his body so that when the brave's long blade came slicing in, the branch took the brunt of the hit. Still the sharp edge sliced past the wood and into the flesh on Stone's exposed chest. A foot-long gash a quarter inch deep appeared along his ribs. The crowd gasped and let out war yells as they began dancing on all sides of the battling pair. Their man clearly was going to win, and win fast.

The half parry of Stone's branch at least managed to send the brave and his machete hurtling about six feet before he could stop himself. Stone fell down from the force of the attack, taking the stick with him. He curled into as tight a ball as he could as he tumbled along the ground. Which was not that tight considering he had a leg with a splint around it to contend with. But all things considered he at least came out of the roll and up to both feet holding the staff in his hands. Dad would have been proud.

Stone took the merest instant to look down at the gash across his chest. He'd live. Just another scar to add to his collection. He whipped his head up and set himself again, making sure the dirt was firm enough beneath his feet so that he could turn fast. Cracking Elk sneered and came in slashing his machete at the air. But this time, perhaps because he'd had a second to get over the insults Stone had hurled at him, he wasn't quite as fast. Just a fraction, perhaps a hundredth of a second slower. But that was all that Stone needed. As the blade came flying in toward his chest, Stone turned his hips with a snap and caught the side of the long knife with the front of the branch. Parry and strike! Parry and strike! How many fucking times had his father pounded that into his head.

But it worked. And it worked again as the brave Indian felt his knife slammed from his grasp as the front end of the thick branch cracked into his wrist. Then before he could even react the other end was swinging up and into his face. He felt it slam into his nose, crushing it into little fragments that danced around inside stretched-out flesh already turning purple. Then he blacked out and slammed facedown right into the earth. It took only an instant for the Indian to shake off the effects of the blow that might have killed most other men. But then he was the chief's son, with the blood of royalty running in his veins.

He let out a whoop and turned himself over fast, pushing his arms down against the ground and preparing to spring up. But he stopped in his tracks. For Stone was standing over him, the branch poised to come down on his skull. One strike and he would be dead, his head opened up, his brains spilling out like the bison's just minutes before. As the entire tribe watched breathless, the chief as well, standing with his eyes big as saucers, Stone just held the staff there like the sword of Damocles, a yard over the Indian's head.

"Kill me, you bastard," Cracking Elk screamed out, waving his fist at Stone. "You won, white man—you with your damned evil dog's powers behind you. No man, especially a paleface, could have beaten me. But the *gods* give you the victory. So kill me! Kill meeeeeee!" He screamed it out, his eyes closed, veins standing out in his neck like worms about to give birth. But Stone just looked down with scorn.

"No, I *won't* kill you. How about that?" he asked with a

laugh, letting the stick lower in his hands. He looked over at
the chief. "Maybe I just won't play your stupid blood
games. Maybe I don't have to follow your rules. Maybe I
don't feel like it." He threw the branch with disgust down on
the ground and stood there balancing on one leg, his face
covered with sweat, his chest and stomach covered with a
sheen of red from the slash.

Cracking Elk looked as if he were going to go mad. His
eyes opened so wide Stone thought they were going to pop
out and he would need two black rocks to put in there. He
opened his mouth, raised his arms to the sky, and let out a
horrible scream of pain and defeat. Then before anyone
could make a move or say a word, the brave, next in line for
the succession of power (or so he had been until that moment), rose and ran screaming like a banshee into the
shadows. Within seconds he had vanished into the darkness,
but his mad whoops and howls could be heard for minutes
slowly dying out in the distance.

## CHAPTER

# Eleven

THERE wasn't a hell of a lot they could do. The tribe
had witnessed it. The gods had witnessed it. Even the
damned Hawk Dog's cousin, which looked like it was ready
to bite anyone who got close, had witnessed it. Stone had
won, at least one battle, and he would live.

"Go!" Chief Buffalo Breaker ordered, pointing with his
finger toward the rubber motel Stone had been staying in.
The chief couldn't even look at the man who had defeated
his son but just stared past him into the roaring bonfire as if

looking for his lost pride. For his son could no longer be his son nor the future chief of the tribe. Cracking Elk was through, finito, kaput. As wiped out in *his* business as a priest caught with an eight-year-old girl in the choir room would be in his. Stone didn't even realize it, but he had in an instant dramatically altered the entire future of the tribe, and the balance of power among its various warring factions.

But ignorance is at least momentary bliss, and Stone grabbed up his crutch and began hobbling back toward the Goodyear teepee with braves falling in on either side. He couldn't help but let a smile dance across his lips. Because he was still alive. And he hadn't expected to be just a minute before.

"Hey, Chief," Stone said, turning his head slightly as he was led off. "How about some food. Not that I care that much, but Hawk Dog here is going to start getting pissed off as hell, I can promise you that. Why, he might even start chewing on some of those tires." He moved forward with a slight hop of enthusiasm that he was still among the living. He didn't see the chief grind his wooden teeth so hard that they made a crunching, cracking sound as wooden splinters fell out of them.

Back at the Rubber Towers Condo, Stone's predictions immediately came true. The dog was in a horrible foul temper, snarling and snapping at everything in sight—Indian ankles, branches along the ground—and when they got inside the tire palace, the walls themselves. It wasn't always like this. But from past experience Stone knew that when the dog had been getting a lot of food for a few days its stomach expanded to quite a large size. And consequently when the source of feasting was removed the stomach took on such a feeling of swollen emptiness that it drove the animal half to madness. It dove headfirst into the back wall of the place, its teeth snapping open and closed like the jaws of a thrashing Great White. Huge chunks of rubber were instantly ripped free and tossed back into the air as if a threshing machine were spitting out black grain.

Stone just sat back and watched in amused amazement as

the animal attacked the thick diesel truck tire as if it were its
mortal enemy, snarling and making a great to-do. Maybe the
crazy mutt had the right idea, Stone decided after a few
minutes of mayhem. At least the damned dog got to release
all its pent-up aggressions this way. Maybe if humanity had
learned to do the same in the past they could have avoided
all the bloodshed and war that seemed to follow them
through history like a swarm of flesh-eating locusts. Yeah,
he could see it now: men, millions, billions of them, all
kicking and shredding and biting at rubber tires. World
peace through the shredding of used tires. Stone knew without question that if the old world were still around he would
have won the Nobel Peace Prize for the idea.

But after about twenty minutes, chow was in fact brought
in by two hard-faced Atsana who glared at Stone as if he
was Judas Iscariot in the Pope's bathroom. Excaliber
stopped in its tracks, a huge piece of black oily rubber in its
mouth. Suddenly it was as if the dog realized where it was,
what it was doing—and the fact that the stinking rubber
tasted like shit. It spat it out, shook its head violently, and
snorted and spat about ten times to rid its mouth and sinuses
of the taste. Then it charged toward the braves like a bull
toward a matador.

The Indians, seeing the Hawk Dog's cousin coming at
them with hunger like pure lust in its eyes, dropped the two
bowls on the ground and tore ass out of there, slamming the
big diesel tires into place with the help of the other men
stationed out front. But the pit bull wasn't interested in Indian flesh. It beelined straight for the still wobbling bowl of
steaming trout stew. The pit bull threw its face into the wide
gourd as if it was going to try to go swimming in it, emerging seconds later with its entire head covered with fish
chunks, vegetables, and river weeds. But the dog looked
quite happy about ingesting its food this way, half through
its mouth, the rest through its ears and fur. It just didn't eat
the way other creatures did.

"Dog, you need a veterinary psychiatrist bad," Stone
grumbled as he hobbled over, got his own bowl of dinner,

and retreated to the far end of the rubber circle about twenty feet off. He didn't want to be too close to the slurping food-storm that was erupting on the far side. But Stone knew that finding a good animal shrink was going to be a little hard in these parts. He tried to eat but found it hard to swallow more than four or five bites. The battle with Crackling Elk had made his stomach feel as if a football team was doing field drills on it. Being milliseconds from death does wonders for the appetite.

Stone was able to fall asleep after about an hour of tossing and turning, trying to find a comfortable position between a cold dirt floor and the hard side of a grooved tractor trailer tire. In his dreams, Stone found to his immense horror that he had to deal with the dog yet again. Only there were dozens of dogs, and they could all fly like the damned Hawk Dog, and they were soaring all around his head like pigeons, snapping out at him and howling as they flew by, trying to bite chunks out of him like the terrier had ripped from the tires. Only Stone wasn't made of rubber. And suddenly he felt teeth on his arm, sinking in, grabbing, ripping.

"Stone Man, wake up, be quiet, be quiet," a voice was saying to him. For a few seconds Stone didn't know if he was still dreaming. There was a hand on his arm, a figure in the semidarkness of the space. He reached forward, grabbed the hand, and started to twist it hard, applying a lock on the wrist. But the shape spoke up.

"No, no, I'm here to help. Stop! The guards will hear us!" Stone kept his own hand on the wrist ready to snap down a hold that could break it in a flash. But he relaxed just a bit and shifted his weight up against the back of the tire so he was at least sitting up, not lying down. The dog remained across the floor sound asleep, abrogating as usual its guard dog responsibilities to the narcotic slumbers of gluttony.

Well, the guy hadn't killed him already, and he sure as hell could have while he was sleeping. In fact, why wake someone just to do him in? Even in his half awake state that made sense, and Stone released his hold so the hand pulled away. He reached with his other for the branch that he kept next to him. No sense being a fool. You never fucking knew.

"I'm not here to harm you, I swear," the voice said out of the darkness. Suddenly, as Stone's eyes got fully opened he saw the face in the dancing shadows from the bonfire in the center of camp as someone had just thrown a pile of fresh dead wood to fuel the flames higher.

"Cracking Elk," Stone whispered in amazement, starting to raise his staff. Surely the man was here to assassinate him after last night.

"Stone Man," the brave said, his face hard as a piece of sheet steel, "I—I'm here to help you escape. I overheard my father and his top advisors talking just minutes ago. They're going to kill you, to avenge the Atsana. It is not permissible that a white man could defeat a brave of our tribe and live. The Hawk Dog's relative—it too must die. Both of you. They will take their chances with the gods."

Stone's mouth dropped yet wider. He didn't know what the hell to believe. "Why the hell are you telling me this, helping me?" Stone asked, his eyes blazing with suspicion. Across the room, the dog heard Stone's voice rising and popped open one eye just a slit to see what was going on, praying that it wasn't something that would entail getting up and going into battle, because it had just found a position that made its swollen stomach stop hurting after hours of gas and pains.

"Because, because . . ." The brave looked down into the darker shadows on the ground. "Because I am a Nadara, a No-Man now. I do not exist. My loss to you destroyed my status in the tribe. I am less than a worm here now and forever. There is no way to regain my self. The Ancient Ways say that a man vanquished in battle must either commit suicide or become a slave to his conquering enemy. I cannot commit suicide, though I wish more than anything that I could, as it is not in the ways of the Atsana. It is a sin beyond sins, beyond even your white hell. So I must become your Natanyi—your—your—" Stone could see how hard it was for the man to say the words, and he felt a sudden pity for the bastard. The guy had been the toughest of the tough in the place, destined for the top, "I cudda been a contender" and all that shit. And now. . .

"Your slave," Cracking Elk said at last, his head bowing down in utter and complete defeat like a man heading down the hall to the execution chamber.

"Hey, lighten up," Stone said, reaching for a small gourd of water on the ground as his lips suddenly felt dry and hot. Maybe he was getting feverish from the leg; it seemed to be throbbing painfully. "But I don't take, need, or want any slaves. You'll have to look for work elsewhere."

"You don't understand. I *must* follow you, by the Law of the Hawk Dog, until *you* or I die. Besides, if you don't get out of here within minutes you're going to be chopped meat anyway," the brave said, and Stone saw the slightest trace of smile at the edges of the hard mouth. The Indian, like his father, looked as if he was chiseled out of the very desert rocks. Stone knew that it was only chance that *he* had won. It had been close, very close.

"Well, that I'll take you up on," Stone said, raising himself up to standing position. Somehow he believed the guy. There was a kind of tragic sincerity about him. As if behind the stoic face that could never show emotion there were so many tears that it was like a dam about to burst, forcing the face to become even harder, more set in concrete, the impenetrable cloudy black eyes motionless as the rocks on the bottom of a crystal stream.

"But how the hell can we get out of here?" Stone asked as he got himself together. "There are guards out there and this place seems impos—"

"The same way I got in," Cracking Elk said, pointing around behind him. Through the grayness Stone could see that one of the bottom tires had been removed without disrupting the rest of the stack above it.

"All right then, let's go," Stone said suddenly. There was no time to fuck around. He hissed the dog's name a few times in the darkness. With a lazy whine the animal declined to get up and turned over on its side away from him.

"Dog, you can stay or go, that's up to you. Give my regards to the chief. I'm sure you'll make a tasty stew for him." With that, Stone turned and followed the brave as he crawled on hands and knees out through the foot-high opening. In a second they were both gone, and the dog, casting bored eyes over that way and seeing them gone, suddenly got the message and jumped to its feet in a flash. The pit bull tore ass straight at the opening, even leaving some food behind, an unprecedented occurrence. It dove at the opening like a third-base runner sliding home.

"This way," Cracking Elk motioned to Stone as they emerged into the flame-flickering predawn darkness outside. "We've got to make our way through a set of inner and then outer camp guards. Then we can go to the river."

"But the river—" Stone began to protest, knowing he couldn't swim in that damned washing machine of brown liquid.

"Stone Man, I told you relax. Indian way. No heart attack. I have boat stashed there," the brave whispered over his shoulder as he led the way forward in a crouch. Stone turned around for a moment to make sure the dog had gotten the message—it had, as it followed along about ten feet behind in low profile, half crawling along as its head scanned back and forth like the radar on a battleship. The day was young. A good battle would work up a fine appetite for some fish, perhaps fish and eggs, in an hour or two. Yes, all things considered the pit bull decided that it was in a good mood, its stomach didn't hurt too much, and it was going to have some fun today. Something it hadn't been getting a hell of a lot of lately thanks to one-legged Chow Boy over there.

Cracking Elk seemed to know exactly what he was doing as he led his two charges from one bush, one tree to another. They moved Indian style through the shadows, blending into the darkness and the rise and fall of the fire. It all worked fine until they were almost at the tree line that led to the river. Suddenly they met two medicine men performing some sort of ungodly spell at this hour of the morning, bent over a small fire pouring pink and purple powders into the flames so they sparkled up like the tail of a roman candle. The two rose and came at the escapees, pulling out long blades. Cracking Elk slammed into his man, knocking him down. But as Stone pulled back his stick to take the sucker's head off, he saw that it was Nanhanke.

There was no time for bullshit like thank yous or good-byes. Yet Stone couldn't just let the guy walk. The chief would suspect something, especially with the other sucker dead, as Stone could see Cracking Elk pulling the brave's own blade from his red chest.

"Sorry," Stone said softly. He let the stick continue on its trajectory down, but aimed it so it glanced off the side of the man's head rather than hitting it full on. The strike did just what Stone hoped it would. It created a lot of blood from the gash, knocked the doc down to the ground in a daze. But it wouldn't do any permanent damage. If anything it would be good for the Medicine Man's career, Stone thought as he turned to follow Cracking Elk into the deeper woods. The man who survived the attack of the gringo and the Hawk Dog's cousin—the Invincible One. Why it would probably lead to the emperorship, the chiefhood, the Chairman of the River Salvage Committee.

"This way," Cracking Elk called softly from the trees. "We've got to move fast. They'll find out soon. My people are clever. They—" But even as he spoke they suddenly heard shouts and then war whoops coming from the camp. The fire roared into life. The hunt was on.

Cracking Elk tore through the brush and the close-packed trees so that they both scraped and cut their arms and had to shield their eyes from the poking branches and thorns. Excaliber, being much lower to the ground, was able to avoid the brunt of the attack, slipping under the lowest branches like doing the limbo. It took only a minute or two and they were out and at the river's edge. Stone stared at the foaming waters and gulped hard. He had to admit it, the damned river scared the shit out of him. He had already been nearly snuffed out in the thing, and now. . .

"Me and my dog ain't the greatest swimmers," Stone

started to protest to Cracking Elk, who again put his fingers to his lips.

"Even a slave can criticize, Stone Man, and I tell you patience is the great virtue and reward. Why, that is the first law of the Hawk Dog. Doesn't your animal even teach you that?" Before Stone could think of an answer, the brave led him to a strange-looking object sitting on the rocky shore. It consisted of about eight diesel truck tires all lashed together to form a sort of rough square shape. And as Cracking Elk began pushing the thing with all his might into the roaring water, Stone realized that it was a boat, or what passed for one around here. Only he didn't like the looks of it at all—the vines holding the damned thing together were all twisted and popping in a lot of places, and some of the rubber on the tires was rotting off, as if they were about to crumble into shreds. The "boat" might once have had some claim to seaworthiness, but that was about twenty years before.

But as Stone saw the flames of numerous torches bouncing through the woods only about fifty yards off, he suddenly decided the tire yacht looked very inviting indeed, and he added his shoulder to the raft. Within seconds they had it into the water, and the current caught it. Suddenly they were all scrambling around trying to get in, Excaliber making a flying leap from the river's edge and just barely catching its front paws on the rapidly departing tire boat. Stone reached around as he lay on his chest half on and half off the thing, and managed to snag the bull terrier's collar with one hand as it kicked away in the water. He gave it a great heave and the animal sort of exploded from the water, landing on one of the tires where it tried to get its balance on the inner rims of the thing.

Stone hoisted himself up just as the first of the Indian posse reached the shoreline. Arrows began flying through the air, but the stiff wind above the river pulled them sharply to the side. He crawled ahead and saw that Cracking Elk was pulling on a long, thick rope that led from one side of the river to the other. It was a ferryboat, Stone suddenly realized, feeling a little dumb. Maybe they were going to get out of this damned thing after all. But even as he rose up on one knee and added his strength to pulling the rope as it passed over the tire raft, so they slowly edged through the river, Stone glanced back as he felt vibrations in the taut rope beneath his arms. The Atsana were chopping away at the thing attached to a tree on the shore, slicing at it as if the rope had just killed their grandmothers. It took only seconds for the cable to be completely severed.

"Shit!" Stone spat out at the aquamarine sky, shimmering like the shell of an oyster above them. For the ferry was already ripping free of the loosened rope and joining the current. Within ten seconds they were moving along at twenty miles an hour and Stone could see, as the craft began rocketing around every which way, that it wouldn't be a hell of a long time before the whole fucking *African Queen* started coming apart at the seams.

## CHAPTER

# Twelve

THEN they were in hell. A wet hell at that. For the huge tire raft was suddenly spinning around, rising ten, fifteen feet in the air and then crashing down again like a surfboard caught in the undertow. When Stone's head emerged from their first submarine dive and he came up coughing, he looked around to see if Cracking Elk were still on for the ride. He saw the Indian at the far end of the raft, his legs wrapped tight around a tire. The brave was grabbing hold of an arrow that was imbedded in his shoulder. With an absolutely expression-less face he ripped the arrow out and threw it into the swirling waters. His head turned forward and up just in time to catch Stone's gaze. He let a smirk ripple across his upper lip as if to say, see how tough the Indian is, white man, a hell of a lot tougher than you are, asshole.

But Stone wasn't arguing, he was just trying to hang on for dear fucking life. He had gone white-water rafting once when about sixteen. But this was different. Aside from the fact that the rafting trip had been for fun and they had all been decked out in heavy life jackets and helmets, the waters had been nothing like this. What had been billed as a "rough water" adventure was like a bathtub compared to the towering waves, the eddies and whirlpools sucking down whole trees into their dark innards.

Stone gripped his legs as hard as he could, as Cracking Elk had done, around a tire beneath him. The raft suddenly rose a good twenty feet in the air, so that Stone could see the whole river ahead for nearly a mile, and then slammed back down into foaming waters like a whale dropped from the sky. Stone could barely hang on even using every bit of his strength. He could feel his whole backbone shake as if it was in a blender, and felt his teeth slam together and threaten to shatter like glass. The pressures on the rising and falling raft were incredible—they must be hitting three and four g's.

The tires strained and pulled at the half-rotted ropes that held them loosely together. Already some of the strands were unraveling, and several of the tires on one end were starting to slap hard a few feet out from the rest of the raft. The thing wasn't going to last a hell of a long time. Not in these waters. After the fourth toss, Stone glanced around just behind him, fearing the worst, but the damned dog was still there, as tenacious as ever, its own legs wrapped around a smaller tire like an octopus trying to strangle a pig. The ride went on unabated for nearly ten minutes as they shot down the river. Stone could see the granite mountains towering on each side of him, spinning around him, making him dizzy. The sun was risen fully now so he could see more clearly. But the foam, the swirling drops and mist kept filling his eyes with water. Suddenly he saw that ahead about a hundred feet the river was narrowing rapidly as the canyon walls pressed in closer from each side. A body of water that had just been hundreds of yards wide was suddenly compressed to the space of about fifty feet, tight between the granite sluices as if forming some kind of aqueduct.

They hit the rough water hard and Stone felt the raft suddenly tear ahead as if supercharged. They were shaken violently, every bone in their bodies vibrating around as if trying to throw the muscles and flesh right off. Then they were accelerating faster as if on a bobsled course hurtling down a hill at 200 mph. The rock walls reached out from both sides, jagged fingers hoping to squeeze their skulls against its hardness.

Suddenly the tire raft slammed right into a boulder and the occupants of the vessel were tossed straight up in the air, all ripped from their holding places. Yet as the currents had it, the raft dropped straight down and stayed absolutely motionless for about three seconds as it just turned around like a slow record turntable. The three of them plopped back down on the rubber and frantically searched for their little holding niches. The funnel effect of the pressing walls seemed to get tighter, making the waters bubble violently as if they were being superheated from below. Just when Stone thought he couldn't hang on another second, just as his grip was slipping away from the wet tire surface, they were suddenly ejected out from between two high rock walls with the striations of ten thousand generations of life cemented inside. The raft dropped about twenty feet and suddenly they were back on a much wider river, the currents instantly dropping to an almost tropical lull.

The raft twisted around like a leaf on a pond as two of the tires broke free and headed their own way. The *Titanic* was going down. They were pushed in close to one shore by a current from the opposite side. Within a minute they were about twenty yards off a sandy shore.

"We're abandoning ship here," the brave shouted from the other end of the raft, cupping his hands over his mouth so he could be heard over the roar of the blasting funnel of white water just a hundred yards behind them.

"But what about the Atsana?" Stone screamed back, not wanting to end up in the hands of the chief, not after he'd seen what the man could do to a buffalo's head. It gave his own skull a headache just to think about it.

"They won't go beyond those narrow canyon walls back there," Cracking Elk reassured him. "It's sacred ground. They think anyone who comes here will die. They won't follow, I'm sure of it." The brave didn't try to explain it all any further but suddenly stood up, dove off into the calm waters, and began swimming over to the sand bank. Stone turned himself over and motioned for the dog to follow him. Which was all well and good, except when he pushed himself off and started trying to swim, Stone found himself sinking like a rock. The splinted leg acted like an anchor on him and even in the slow-moving waters it was too much. The Indian, who had just been pulling himself up on shore, turned and saw Stone disappearing beneath the surface only about twenty-five feet out.

He dove straight back into the water, and paddling like an Olympic prospect was at the drowning man's side in seconds. Stone felt a hand around his collar and suddenly he was being pulled backwards on the surface of the river. He took a few deep sputtering breaths and felt himself being dragged up onto the sand. Cracking Elk collapsed on the shore beside him, gasping for breath himself from the exertions. Stone, after coughing up, sat up and caught sight of the dog, bedraggled and pissed-off as hell, crawling up onto the sand about fifty feet down. It looked like a sewer rat, with its fur all slicked down, ears back in defensive mode. Life with the Chow Boy was daily taking a turn for the worse.

"Thanks," Stone managed to sputter to the brave. The Indian wouldn't utter a word or make the slightest expression as Stone turned to him to express his gratitude. If anything the brave didn't seem to like the idea that he had just saved Stone. Yet he was his slave, bound to serve the man at every turn, a man whom he would just as soon have seen a moldering corpse in the dirt. But then Stone wasn't particular about who saved his ass. He'd already been rescued from the great beyond by whores, prospectors, paraplegics, deaf mutes. A stonefaced Indian was just one addition to the club.

CHAPTER

# Thirteen

STONE'S splint arrangement had come completely undone in all the goings-on, and he spent about five minutes retying everything, getting the sticks back in place. It seemed infected all around the break, though it was hard to tell for sure. Still he could feel it mending, knitting together inside of him, strength slowly seeping back into the limb. But it would be weeks, maybe months before it was fully functional. That was all he needed out here in the jungles of America, where the slightest indication of weakness was usually rewarded by something snapping out from behind a bush to kill and/or eat the wounded thing which was showing itself to be vulnerable. Stone wished he were carrying a fucking bazooka, instead of a piece of wood six feet long.

He wanted to rest up for a few more minutes but Cracking Elk was on his feet, walking impatiently in a tight circle in the sand.

"Come on, come on, got to go. Go now!" He looked at Stone somewhat contemptuously, pulling his lips back as if it were difficult for the Indian to even talk to the white man.

"I thought you said the rest of the tribe wouldn't come in

here because of bad medicine," Stone said wearily, not wanting to rise for at least a hundred years.

"Not tribe—other things. Very dangerous all through here. Other braves never return, all die."

"Oh, it's just superstition," Stone said, trying to gain a few more minutes by moving his lips instead of his feet. "Just propaganda to keep you all locked up there on that two-mile-long stretch of shoreline called home."

"No, it's more than that," Cracking Elk said, not able to meet Stone's eyes. "There is darkness, evil in these parts. We must be careful. And we must"—he looked up at the heavens, judging the time from the color of the now misted and luminous sky—"make good time. I want to be on higher ground downriver before dark. There are places we shouldn't be caught out at night." But suddenly as if he'd already said too much Cracking Elk stopped talking, turned, and began walking slowly through the sand along the river's edge. There was a dark fire in his eyes—hate, murder. The brave's whole life had been turned upsidedown in twenty-four hours: from the top of the heap to a piece of useless garbage with not even a home or a people anymore. He hated Stone more than he'd ever hated any man in his life. Yet the brave was bound to the laws of the Atsana that had been laid down by the very animal gods themselves. He was Stone's slave until he or the white man died. He would serve him, but he would hate him every second of his servitude.

"Oh for Christ's sake," Stone mumbled, hobbling up onto one foot as he got his balance with a new makeshift crutch, a not very straight piece of branch that had been washed up on the shore next to him in the sand. "I'm coming, I'm coming." He stumbled along like Tiny Tim in *A Christmas Carol* as the pit bull took up a miserable third place, just hoping a squirrel or some damn thing came scampering by so it could take a nice bite and get rid of its foul mood. The animal wasn't into diets.

The going was fairly easy at first, just sandy shoreline about twenty feet wide, almost white, clean looking, like something you'd find at Miami Beach. Stone kept glancing over at the river, which roared alongside them, now stretched back out to a width about a hundred feet of raging brown. The remains of whatever had gone through the rapids and rocks back there came bobbing along—mostly animal and fish carcasses, all bloated with heads smashed in as their skulls had been pounded against the rocks. Stone had just been close as a hair on an ant's balls to that very fate himself.

But after about two miles the going got harder, with sharp little rocks like punji sticks all over the place. It was difficult for all of them—the Indian in his moccasins, Stone with the crutch unable to get a good grip on the slippery stones, and the pit bull with its slipping and sliding paws suited for many things but not clambering along on ten million wet and pointy rocks. But soon Stone wished the rocks were back again as they came to bogs, soft mud that the feet sank into the moment they were placed down. They sludged along keeping within grasp of each other just in case someone started actually going under. And the legs of a goat poking up from the scum-covered mud off to one side as if the thing was frozen in an eternal kick of rigor mortis were an indication that their concerns were justified.

But it was the dog who found the soft spot first. They both suddenly heard a terrible squealing behind them and turned to see the pit bull going under fast. It had strayed too close to the departed goat and looked about to join it. Already the animal was down to its chest, all four legs disappearing beneath the white sucking sand. The dog looked terrified, its ears pointing straight up. And the sound it made was truly horrific.

"Jesus fucking Christ," Stone snarled as he started backtracking as fast as he could. But at the rate the damned dog was slipping under, it would just be a memory within a minute.

"Hold on," Cracking Elk shouted as he put his arm up to stop Stone from venturing out onto the dog-eating sand. "Lie down, reach out for it like on ice—I'll hold your legs." The idea of getting his face down into the muck was unappealing to say the least. But Stone lay down and squirmed ahead through the sand as Cracking Elk dropped flat and grabbed hold around his ankles. Within seconds Stone was just within reach of the dog, which was looking at him with a most pitiful expression, only its head now above the sand. It knew it had fucked up bad.

"Hang on, dog, just hang on," Stone screamed as he reached into the muck trying to find some part of it to grab. Just as the hapless animal's head completely vanished beneath the sucking sands Stone grabbed something—the dog's right leg—and pulled back with all his might. Stone gripped with everything he had and yanked his arm back toward him. It was incredibly hard going, like ripping something out of setting concrete.

"Pull," Stone screamed out to Cracking Elk, lying on his stomach right behind him. "I've got it—pull me, man, fast. I think I'm starting to slide into this shit myself." It seemed at first as if the dog wasn't going to budge even with both men exerting all their energy. But suddenly the pit bull popped right up onto the surface, coughing and spitting a storm of mud from its mouth. Stone pulled back hard at the same time the Indian wriggled backwards dragging Stone by his ankles. Within twenty seconds they were all deposited on less shifting sands, covered with the slimy muck. The dog shook itself violently, spraying most of the dirt onto them, and looked at the two men who had just rescued it and let out with an ear-cracking little whine, as if it knew how fucking close it had just been—and well, thanks guys . . . I know I can be an asshole but . . .

"No rest," Cracking Elk said after about sixty seconds. "It will be this way all the way downriver. Every mile holds danger. We've got to keep on, never stop except when we drop. To slow here is to die." Stone was starting to believe the bastard. The whole river valley had an eerie, dangerous quality about it as if it existed only to destroy living things —take them down in its watery grasp, smash them against its rocks, grip them in sandy jaws and take them to asphyxiating deaths. The Indian was right. They'd better get through here as fast as they could travel. Stone had no illusions: he was the one slowing the whole fucking game down.

But it was Cracking Elk who ran into the next bit of trouble. And when it came, it came like a rocket blasted from a hidden silo. He had just walked over to a tree about thirty feet from shoreline, thinking he saw the carcass of a small animal, when a shape launched itself from a bush nearby and came right at the Indian like a mini tank: a warthog, only slightly larger than Excaliber, but a solid sheath of muscle and tusks a good twelve inches long, which looked as sharp as assault bayonets. The brave jumped straight up in the air, driven by sheer fear to leap a good four feet off the ground and right over the thing's charging tusks and back.

The creature was ugly as sin, Stone could see as it slowed itself fast and turned for the second charge. Its face was a huge snout with great teeth bigger than the pit bull's, and immense tusks that looked like they could cut through steel, all set atop a small but extremely powerful body covered with a coarse layer of dark matted fur. The creature stank to high heaven, a walking musk factory, as it wheeled around seeking the man it had just missed. But Excaliber was just as fast. With a growl, the pit bull caught the warthog's attention and the wild animal froze. As all porkers are, it was smart as shit, and this hog was more clever than most. And mean too. It snarled back and decided that the pit bull was more of a danger than the man it had started after. Jumping straight off the dirt and wheeling around in midair with amazing grace and speed for such an ugly little fucker, the warthog made a ninety-degree turn and charged toward the pit bull.

But the distraction that the terrier had created was all that Stone needed. For as the wild pig ran by him hardly noticing him standing there almost motionless Stone brought the branch crutch down with all his might. The stick slammed into the warthog's head with a sickening crack and the animal stopped in its tracks as if it had just run into a brick wall. Its whole body shook all over with rapid, violent quivers. But Stone wasn't going to give it a chance to get a second wind. He raised the stick again and brought it down even harder. This time a huge crack appeared in the side of the animal's skull and red shot out like maple syrup from a tree. Still the warthog wouldn't go down and even as Excaliber started toward it, his jaws stretched wide, the hog stomped its front hoof in the dirt and prepared to charge again.

Stone raised the stick one more time and brought it down with every ounce of strength left in his racked body. This time the stick crashed right into the top of the skull and the warthog dropped, all four knees giving out at once. It lay there unquestionably finished, what with brain spurting out of a huge crack in the head like yolk from a broken egg. The body shook as if an electric current was going through it. The Indian went down on one knee and quickly sliced out a whole section of the tenderest and most nutritious meat from the side of the beast and wrapped it in leaves. Then not even looking back as the creature went into its final death spasms, the two men and a dog headed down the river, wondering just what the hell was going to come after them next.

They walked until it started growing dark. At last as the sun fell like a wounded bird from a sky all blood red and oozing, Cracking Elk said, "It's time to stop. We must build a fire to keep the night stalkers away. There are many here."

"You don't have to convince me," Stone replied, dropping down to his good knee as he huffed away madly. "That Night of the Living Porkchop back there convinced me of anything bad you want to say about this cursed place." The Indian turned his back on Stone as if he didn't want him to see what he was doing. The brave fiddled around with his hands and presto, within a couple of minutes he had a small fire built up of dry weeds and twigs.

"So Indians really can make fire from rubbing two sticks together?" Stone asked in friendly fashion as he walked over and sat down in front of the warming rays of the fire. It was the first warm thing he had felt all day except for the stinking hot breath of the charging hog.

"We have our ways," Cracking Elk replied, as poker-faced as ever, not even looking at Stone's face. He never seemed to look right into the white man's face—as if it was too painful to confront the man who had destroyed his rep—as if Stone might see the lust for murder that burned just beneath the surface like a raging storm in the brave's heart. He took out the strips of pork steak he had carved from the recently deceased and within minutes the delicious scent of roast pig was wafting over them all. They ate the mass of meat, the dog, needless to say, slurping up everything that wasn't tied down.

Stone swore that even the pit bull would be filled up after the feast of charcooked pig, but as they prepared to go off to sleep, lying in the dirt on little leaf and twig beds they had quickly built, the dog somehow caught a bat flying in wild circles above the fire. It crunched the little black mammal between its teeth, killing it in a single bite. Then the two men had the supreme pleasure of listening to the animal gnaw on the bat for hours, crunching each wing, each bone, chewing on the thing lustily as if it might never eat again.

# CHAPTER

# Fourteen

STONE hadn't the foggiest idea what time it was when he was awakened. But it was late. The hour of the doomed, somewhere between the end of the night and sunrise. A limbo of time in which the vilest of creatures walk the face of the earth and claim it for their own. Suddenly Stone heard again the sound which had awakened him. A joining together of numerous voices? Howls? Stone didn't know what the hell they were. But he knew he didn't like them. There was something dark in them. Something that promised blood.

"What the hell is that?" Stone asked through the darkness as he saw that Cracking Elk was awake, his eyes wide open, sitting up and listening.

"I—I don't know," the Indian answered. And even in the darkness Stone could see that the brave was scared. "We've heard the sounds far away sometimes when out hunting early in the morning. But never this close. They can't be more than a mile from here."

"They? What are they?" Stone asked, feeling that the Indian was reluctant to say more but in fact knew a hell of a lot more.

"Demons," Cracking Elk answered with a look of supernatural awe. "Ntani—the clawed ones." He made a sign over his chest with both hands, not dissimilar to a Catholic crossing himself, only this was two circles in opposite directions.

The sound rose again, and this time it made the hairs on the back of Stone's neck rise up like little quills and stay there. The sound was unearthly. He had never heard anything even remotely like it. Excaliber too had now risen up onto all fours, pointing toward the sound. The dog didn't like it either: its fur bristled and its jaws seemed to grind against one another as if sharpening the teeth within for trouble ahead.

The men tried to go back to sleep, to ignore it, and the dog as well, once it saw that they weren't heading out. The three of them lay there trying to count sheep, count wampum, count bones, whatever. But it was a joke. How could you sleep when the choirs of hell were practicing right down the fucking road. As he lay still, Stone started distinguishing between different wails within the cacophonous siren of sound. After half an hour with not the slightest diminishing of noise he sat up again. The Indian was already up, kneeling as if in meditation, listening hard.

"Let's go check it out," Stone said, looking firmly at the

brave. "I'd rather see whatever the hell is out there before it sees us. If we're in danger perhaps we can plan some countermeasures."

"Yes," Cracking Elk replied opening his eyes. "We must see." With that he rose up from his crouch and smacked the dirt off his buckskin pants and jacket. Stone rose with somewhat more difficulty, cursing to himself. He hated being crippled. It made a hard world a hell of a lot harder. Stone glanced over to the other side of the smoldering fire, just a few orange coals glowing beneath the dark gray ash. The dog was sound asleep. Having seen that the human crew wasn't about to check things out earlier, it had assumed that that was it for the night and had gone into heavy hibernation. Just as well, Stone thought as he hobbled off behind the Indian. They didn't need the damned dog charging into some pack of whatever the hell was out there and setting the demonic crew on them all.

Stone followed Cracking Elk in the near darkness, lit with only a dim, dark purplish light that trickled down from above as night hung on and dawn struggled to make even a dent of light in the eastern sky. It was rough over the rocks along the shore but at least no brambles which had torn Stone's arm and chest to shreds the day before. The Indian went at near full speed, and Stone had to hobble along like a one-legged maniac with his ass on fire to keep up.

The screams and howls grew louder and louder, until it was deafening, taking up their entire senses like the roar of a jet or the passage of a screaming subway train. Only these were not things made of steel but living beings, a chorus of madness in rising crescendo that seemed as if it was trying to wake the very dead. The Indian came to a stop along the shore and made a sharp right, heading toward the solid mountain wall that rose up a thousand feet, about a hundred feet away. But as Stone followed, once again going through bramble bushes so his just-beginning-to-heal rips and tears from the day before were again torn asunder, he saw that there was a much lower ridge about a hundred feet up. The angle was easy enough for even Stone to ascend with the aid of his walking stick.

Halfway up he nearly tripped over something: bones! And in the minimal starlight from the billion galaxies burning dimly above, he could see that there were bones everywhere along the hill. It was a fucking graveyard, or a garbage dump. The brave moved slower and slower as he reached the top of the rise. Whatever the hell was on the other side, the last thing he wanted was for it to spot them. Stone, with much the same thoughts in mind, winced as he climbed, for the choruses of yowling were actually causing pain to his ears, making them ache as if icepicks were being slammed inside. Both men reached the top, a rocky ledge about twenty feet wide, slid across it on their stomachs—and looked down onto the other side. Looked down onto the living hell unfolding a hundred feet below them in a small valley bounded on each side by rocky cliffs several hundred feet high. Looked down and prayed silently to their respective gods to protect them from the dark goings-on.

Dogs, hundreds of them, jumping and leaping about in the grayness, throwing themselves with abandon into the air and then crashing down, smashing into one another with loud thuds. They spun wildly about, launching themselves every which way, all howling and yapping, barking and snarling at once. The center of the mad dance appeared to be a tree that had been struck by lightning and was burning brightly in the center of the valley floor. With its outstretched branches it formed a sort of triangular cross around which the dogs raced and jumped in total madness.

As Stone settled down even further, pressing his face against the edge of the plateau, he could see that though some were just leaping around, others were fighting, clawing and biting furiously at one another. Many already had huge chunks of their flesh ripped out, their pelts splattered with bright red. Others' jaws were blood soaked, bits of dog flesh hanging out in jagged pieces. And yet not one seemed to mind. Those that were bitten yowled out in mortal pain, but they didn't run off or try to hide. Far from it, they seemed to wear their bloody holes as patches of honor, parading them, joining in the insane frenzied death of the hundreds of dogs.

There were many large dogs, and these seemed to prey on the smaller ones like sharks on fish. They leaped about high in the air—dobermans, shepherds, even a few mastiffs here and there, jumping back and forth wildly like African dancers acting out a Busby Berkley routine. They attacked the smaller dogs, the collies and dachshunds, the poodles and miniatures, knocking them down like bowling pins, grabbing them in their teeth and throwing them high in the air like bloody beachballs so the animals tumbled back to earth with high-pitched squeals of terror. Yet again, when they touched down—if they were still alive—they joined in the racing circle again around the blazing tree like some sort of canine Mecca.

As the narrow sky above started turning a dark shade of purple, Stone could see even deeper into the bloody spectacle. In front of the blazing tree stood three dogs, side by side like kings, rulers, emperors of the fur. They were immense animals, each a worthy example of its breed. A doberman, a labrador—and one of Excaliber's own—a pit bull, with a back that a table could be rested on. The three dogs, in sharp contrast to the rest of the maddened bloodthirsty animals, seemed completely possessed of their faculties and watched coldly as the procession circled around them. From time to time they turned to one another, and though Stone couldn't hear anything above the deafening din of the snarling and screaming animals, he swore they were "discussing" the situation. *That*, more even than the horrors he saw evolving below, gave Stone chills that only a corpse should have to endure.

As his eyes roamed the blood party he saw behind a tree one final piece of the canine ritual that his eyes had missed thus far: a wading pond of blood. The smaller dogs that had been decimated, annihilated and ground up into burger had been thrown back here. And after dozens had been deposited the ground had become saturated with a pool of thick blood,

nearly fifteen feet in diameter, bubbling away like a little
volcano. As the concentric spinning circles of creatures
came around the back of the tree they rushed to the red lake
and lapped it up, drank in great gulps of the thick liquid.
Many ran through the red stuff, played in it, rolled around
and around so that when they emerged they were coated,
painted in the color of life—and death. They were mon-
strous dripping mops of red fur as they rushed back out and
rejoining their racing comrades.

Stone and the Indian turned and looked at one another
with expressions of pure horror on their faces. Stone saw
real fear on the brave's face now. Even Indians have their
breaking point. Cracking Elk put his lips to Stone's ear.
"There is also the opposite of the Hawk Dog, the Vulture
Dog. Like those below. We must leave—now. This is an
evil, evil place. If they find us they'll—they'll—." The Indian didn't have to convince Stone. He was ready to dive
back in the fucking river to get away from this crew.

But they had barely pulled back a foot down the slope
when they heard a loud barking coming from just feet away.
Both men's heads turned as one and in the now violet rays of
the new morning they could see a dog six yards to the right,
perched on the very edge of the precipice that looked down
over the demonic scene of canine sacrifice and blood wor-
ship. It was Excaliber.

"Shit," Stone groaned to himself. If the worst thing that
could possibly happen were to happen, this was it. And even
as they watched, the pit bull let loose with a howling challenge to the massess below. Its head rose up to the slowly
lightening sky so it formed a perfect silhouette, as did the
two men still perched on their elbows at the very edge.

And that was enough. For suddenly one of the three giant
dogs in the center of the bloody scene saw the shapes on the
rise above them. It rose up on its hind paws, a terrifying
vision nearly seven feet high with the burning branches of
the tree behind it, and let out with its own screaming howl of
pure authority. The entire dance of death stopped in its tracks
and every single dog was instantly silent, even those bleed-

ing from gaping wounds in their sides. They all feared The
Three even more than pain or death itself. And as Stone's
heart fell right down into his stomach, where it proceeded to
boil itself in digestive fluids, the three leaders pointed with
their heads up at the intruders and let out with a combined
howl of challenge that echoed back and forth along the valley walls like thunder. And then every fucking dog that
could still move came in one great mass of teeth, paws, and
burning bloodthirsty eyes straight toward Martin Stone and
his favorite animal.

## CHAPTER

# Fifteen

HAVING two hundred snarling, snapping, salivating
dogs lunging up at you with a hatred that only crunching your bones in half will release was not exactly the way
Martin Stone felt like starting the day. The only good thing
was that as hard as they tried, as hard as they flung themselves against the mountain slope a hundred feet below the
men and their errant dog, the dog pack just couldn't get up
the thing more than twenty or thirty feet at most before tumbling back to earth with painful yelps as they bounced along
the rocks below them.

The dogs had come into the valley from the far side,
nearly two miles around to get back to the river's edge. But
as the three leaders joined in a howl in unison they got the
entire pack to stop its useless scramblings at the wall and led
them at full speed off in the opposite direction. The migra-
tion, barking and howling away like a locomotive made of
fur, exited through the woods.

"Damn dog!" Stone snarled over at the pit bull as the three of them shot down the hill they had just climbed. "Why couldn't you have stayed back in camp chewing on your fucking bat or something?" But Stone could see, as he looked at the dog with its front legs straight and stiff as it slid on its ass right down the sandy hill, that the pit bull looked a little green around the gills too, realizing—after the fact—that perhaps it hadn't done the cleverest thing back up there. Not that repentance was going to help matters.

They all hit the bottom of the slope at just about the same time, and with the dust still rising around them they took off down the shoreline, one Indian, one crutch-swinging cripple, and one overmacho dog shooting along the sand like gazelles in full flight. The image of those wild dogs with fangs glistening in the dawn light was all that any of them needed to fuel their strides.

It was rough going. Either they had to run along the rocks near the tree line, or by the river on the sand that was so soft that their feet kept sinking down two or three inches as if into snow. The three of them hopped back and forth from one to another as they got alternately exasperated with each mode of travel. As they ran the dawn fell fully from the sky with a sudden explosion of vibrant color. Off in the distance they could hear the barking and howling of the blood-maddened pack, and though it wasn't yet close it sure as hell wasn't moving off.

The pain was agonizing every time Stone put any weight on the broken leg. But finally figuring out the use of the crutch after a few days practice, he was able to get his leg and the branch in some sort of synchronization with one another so that he was galloping right along like a bionic racehorse, nearly keeping up with the Indian. The pit bull took up the rear, running just behind Stone, stopping every few minutes to check out just what the hell was happening behind them. Its ears pivoted as it sniffed suspiciously at the wind, checking out the surroundings for danger.

Thus it was the dog that caught the forward squad of attackers coming in at twelve o'clock. The pit bull had just slowed to make a danger check, turned to take a look over its shoulder, and nearly busted a gut. For shooting along like rocket cars rather than something made of muscle and blood were just under half a dozen greyhounds. They were thin, all bone and legs, but huge, and tearing like a pack of cheetahs. The animals were the fastest dogs yet bred, and they flew in with such speed that even Excaliber, which considered itself something of a quick draw, had only a chance to let off with a single warning bark to the men ahead before it turned to face the first comer.

Usually the pit bull's tactics were to charge into the enemy, but it had barely gotten its front legs in gear when one of the suckers came flying right into it like a defensive back trying to take it out. The pit bull, seeing that it couldn't charge, froze its body solid as a rock as it saw the mass of flying fur, the jaws open wide waiting for contact. Setting its front legs and aiming its head down, the dog made an almost immovable object as the lead greyhound soon found. It ran right into the solid wall of fur and snapped down hard with its jaws, only to find itself munching empty space. Then it was flying through the air right over the pit bull, soaring past with its scrawny long legs pumping the air like a swimmer who doesn't know how to swim.

Stone and Cracking Elk heard the pit bull's warning bark and stopped in their tracks, both men's eyes opening wide as the band of greyhounds came flying along the beach, their long legs taking bounding leaps a good ten to twelve feet at a time. If the rest of the pack was right behind them, then Stone and his crew were all dead. But if it was just a forward scouting party—and the greyhounds were probably twice as fast as the rest—then they might have a chance. Might! For already two of the magnificent animals were wading into Excaliber, the rest tearing ass toward the two men. And the huge black-faced son of a bitch in the lead was coming straight at Stone, looking at his face like it was the King-Sized Super Greyhound Meat Treat, the canine's favorite.

"Not tonight, you bastard," Stone screamed, letting his

own voice challenge the howls and barks of the attackers. He swung his branch around just as the greyhound leaped, its jaws opened like a bear trap. Only Stone's stick hit the center of its face first. The whole nose and jaw of the animal just sort of disintegrated in a mucky mess of blood, fur, and teeth. Stone let the animal fly past him, slamming into the ground with a horrible wet thud, without even a second glance. The dead were the ants' problem, the living were his.

Cracking Elk had run forward to help Stone, but found two of the overtoothed attackers doing their airborne thing toward him. But the Indian was tough, very tough—he had killed many animals and a few men in his life. He moved with an equal lightning speed, ducking under the lead dog as it came at him. He slammed the machete straight up so it ripped right into the stomach of the animal, slicing it from chest to crotch as the flying dog's own motion did the cutting. Organs, intestines, all kinds of slurping and throbbing pieces of meat came flying out over Cracking Elk, covering his head and shoulders. When the dog came down on the ground ten feet past him, the jarring landing ripped out whatever the hell else was left inside—lungs, pancreas, heart. The dog slapped down into the dirt with a sickening wet splat like a pancake thrown from a skyscraper.

But the brave didn't have time to admire his handiwork. The second greyhound was at him, its jaws coming right at the Indian's neck. It was only by lifting his shoulder fast at the last instant that the Indian was able to take the blow in his upper arm rather than his throat. Not that that felt too great either. The teeth sank deep into the muscle and the bone, the greyhound setting there like a snapping turtle around a fish. Cracking Elk fell to the ground in a tumble of fur and blood. Suddenly his knife was knocked from his hand and he knew that the jig was close to up. He tried to push the creature off but it was too strong, too wild. Suddenly it loosened its grip on his shoulder for an instant, turned, and came down right toward his face, the snapping jaws gushing with saliva and his own blood as they came toward him.

But at the very instant the brave was preparing to go to the Not-So-Happy Hunting Grounds he heard a loud *thwack*, felt a shuddering, and suddenly the dog was dead weight on top of him. As he slid it off, the brave saw Stone, the stick hefted in his hands, turning away again to meet the next crazed canine that was coming in like he was on a kamikaze mission. Whatever spell the three lead dogs had over these animals was unreal. They were willing to do anything, including giving up their lives, to carry out the orders of the pack's top brass. Was this how it was going to be: mutant dogs with super intelligence? Stone prayed it wouldn't be, but he didn't have time to dwell on it all as yet another pair of thrashing jaws was heading for his nose.

Excaliber meanwhile had his teeth full. It wasn't that on a one-on-one he couldn't have taken on these dudes all fucking day, but the bastards didn't want to fight fair. The first one came at him and he disposed of it quickly with two sharp bites to the throat artery, leaving it lying in a pool of its own hot blood. Then the next two came in together, one from each side, both of their jaws open to the max like anacondas preparing to swallow a whole cow. But the dog had plans of his own. He charged at the one on his left, then slipped down to the ground so he slid under it as the flying brick wall of fur came at him. It was the oldest trick in the book, but it worked every fucking time. Dogs weren't prepared for strategy, for flanking, for slipping punches. But that was the only way Excaliber knew how to play the game —with no rules.

The two attackers met head on, their jaws closing on each other's faces. And as the pit bull stood back with a most satisfied look, they bit away at one another for a good four or five seconds before the bloody animals realized what they were doing. By the time they swung their attention back to the pit bull, he was the hunter and *they* the hunted. He rushed around them in a circle trying to tie up their feet, make them dizzy. In a flash like a rattler striking, he lunged in and slammed his teeth around one of their front paws. With a single bite the bone cracked like a piece of balsa wood and the pit bull spat it out, jumping backward before the second dog could make a move.

Stone and Cracking Elk had but one dog left to contend with between them. The animal snarled first at one then the other, unsure of which man to take on as they stood about six feet apart and taunted it. Suddenly the greyhound made some sort of decision and leaped at the Indian. It was its last mistake. For at the very instant it hit the air Stone swung upward with all his might with the branch, catching the thing full in the chest. As it rocketed upward squealing, its front ribs broken like bad lathing, the Indian slammed his knife forward and down. The combined energy of the two strikes pushed the machete into the animal's neck with such force that the head was instantly guillotined. The dog shot past the brave, its head flying in one direction, its body in another. It sailed into death one mixed up son of a bitch.

The men turned back to see who the next fool was that wanted them, but there were no more takers, just the pit bull facing down his scraggly, blood-soaked opponent. The last one left. The animal whined a most pitiful kind of sound. It had felt tough minutes before, but seeing its compatriots turned into compost had done something to the animal's confidence level. As Excaliber growled and started in, the greyhound decided that it had had enough. It turned tail and ran, putting all of its remaining strength into getting a jump on the pit bull, which it didn't have to go very far to do. For the bull terrier, seeing that things were basically over except for the medal ceremonies, let itself relax, tongue snapping up and down from its mouth like a broken venetian blind as the dog suddenly let its tiredness show.

"Let's go," the Indian said. "No time for trophies. Those are scouts. One got away and now they know exactly where we are." They started back down the shoreline, jumping over the still twitching greyhounds, broken like bloody dolls all over the place. The morning sun was breaking through, lighting the surrounding mountains, the river, and trees with a crystal whiteness. Not that the dogs needed to see: they could smell ten thousand times better than humans. But it would help Stone, who was able to move a lot faster, being able to spot holes and rocks along his path. He realized that the further ahead he placed the crutch the faster he could move. And once he saw what obstacles lay around him, he was able to zip along so that at some points, on straight-aways, he actually pulled ahead of the Indian, who was running at about three-quarters full speed.

But it couldn't go on like this. Not when they stopped on a rise and could see the pack just two miles or so behind them, a blur of racing bodies coming at them like an invading army, a blitzkrieg of claws and jaws.

"There," the brave said, pointing toward the solid rock wall about fifty yards off. "A ledge, maybe twenty feet above the ground. If we can—"

"If we can—" Stone muttered skeptically. But he was already following the brave, who made a sharp turn and was heading through the omnipresent bramble bushes. They reached the base of the mountain, which seemed to rise up like a mythical castle into the sky glowing overhead. Cracking Elk had seen right: there was a ledge, about fifteen, not twenty, feet above. But how the hell did they get up? The same almost sheer rock wall that would keep the dog pack from scrambling up the side made it just about unclimbable for them as well.

"Here, Stone Man, quick—on my shoulders," the Indian said, kneeling down right against the side of the wall. "I'll push you up. Then you reach down and—"

Stone threw his walking/killing stick up onto the ledge, getting it up, thank God, with one heave. He leaned forward and stepped up onto the brave's shoulders with his good leg. The Indian stood up, grunting with the task of lifting the 180-pound-plus Stone straight up into the air. But the brave was strong, having spent a lifetime hunting, carrying two-hundred-pound carcasses of deer and elk back to camp on his shoulders. It was more Stone's problem, once he was standing up, to get enough of a handhold above to pull himself up. With his stiff splinted leg that acted like a dragging weight slamming against the rock, Stone, using only arm strength, pulled with everything in him, slowly, agonizingly slowly, onto the ledge.

Suddenly he was up and he flopped over the top. He made a quick scan with his eyes to make sure there was nothing waiting to do them in. But the place was deserted. Stone swung around, reaching out his arm, setting himself with the other arm against some boulders right at the edge of the ledge. Cracking Elk couldn't quite reach with his outstretched fingers, but taking a little run he jumped up and caught hold around the outstretched hand. Stone's arm felt as if it was being pulled right out of its socket. But he held on. He had to, for as his face contorted with pain he could see that the front ranks of the pack were already at the long stretch of sand that began about half a mile down the river one. There were only minutes left.

He let out a half scream and pulled hard, and suddenly Cracking Elk was climbing right up the side of his arm like it was a vine. In another second or two the brave was up and over the side. Now there was just one left, and it didn't look like he was going to make it. The pit bull was turning around in anxious circles on the ground just below them. He could see and hear the enemy coming in like a deafening horde of locusts. Only these locusts had teeth and would rip him to shreds in an instant. That, even the virtually fearless pit bull knew. The dogs reached the shoreline level with the ledge and turned in such a sharp angle that the front ranks half skidded along the sand and tumbled out of control.

Stone looked around desperately and spotted the walking pole. He grabbed it and lowered one end until it was about six feet from the ground.

"Jump, you mangy bastard, jump!" Stone screamed out in his most commanding tones. The dog got the idea, and setting its legs back sprang up like something launched from a trampoline. But it misjudged the angle of flight and cracked right into the side of the mountain, falling back down again as it completely missed the stick.

"Oh God," Stone groaned from between his teeth as he saw the dogs coming down the open space to the mountainside just yards away. The pit bull took one more look, prayed to its dog gods, and set its legs for what it knew would be its last try on this particular event. The dog jumped just as a huge doberman launched itself out of the front ranks. Excaliber caught hold of the front end of the thick staff and clamped his teeth around it like a vise around a piece of pipe. No way in hell those teeth were coming unclamped from that wood. Stone pulled with all his might like a fisherman who had just hooked a sea monster, and could hardly raise the animal, which dangled in the air right over the howling hordes that jumped up snapping at its tail. The Indian threw himself forward and grabbed with both hands around the stick. Together they pulled, and their combined power suddenly lifted the animal like it was being shot from a catapult. It rose up into the air and then over their heads, slamming into the wall at the back of the ledge about ten feet behind them.

But they were safe, at least for the moment. The dogs below howled and charged at the wall, snapping up into the air. They jumped and leaped about like the flame tongues of a vast fire. Ten thousand pounds of dog meat and dagger-sharp teeth came flying into the air, like missiles seeking to rip out the faces of those above them.

"Man's best friend?" Stone snorted as he fell back, gasping for breath on the rocky surface. "Those dudes got some bad attitude problems. Must have had the Marquis de Sade for their fucking trainer."

# Sixteen

IF looks could kill, then Stone, the Indian, and wonderdog were all dead as proverbial doorknobs. For after the dogs spent a good ten minutes charging up to the rock wall, smashing against the mountain, they slowly realized that they couldn't reach the three climbers. And this drove them to even more infuriated heights so that they began biting one another. They probably would have consumed each other down to the last tail, given enough time. But the Three showed up—the three immense canines, the rulers of this particular band of monstrosities.

The Three weren't even moving fast, just trotting along side by side with a contingent of guards, huge malamutes that ran along on each side. The dogs moved with ease and arrogance as if the entire world was waiting for their arrival. They reminded Stone of three rulers from the old world: Mussolini, Franco, and Hitler. He remembered seeing a newsreel once of the three bloated murderers meeting, all smiles, stiff salutes, and standing around in tough poses, hands on hips. If he wasn't most probably going to be eaten alive in the next hour or two Stone might have found the whole theater amusing. But it wasn't. Not at all.

The Three walked up to an open area in front of the ledge where the two humans and Excaliber sat looking down, their hearts still beating like war drums on the Mohawk. The other dogs cleared a way for the Three, stumbling out of the way, lurching off as if their paws were on fire, letting out shrill yaps of terror as they rushed to each side, tails between their legs. The power of the trio of dogs over the rest of the pack was quite extraordinary.

They looked down at the three dogs. The dogs looked up at them. And no words needed to be said. Stone fixed his eyes on the Three: the Doberman, huge and sleek, with muscles like steel cables crisscrossing its brown body; the Labrador, big as a lion, its thick black coat hanging down like a musk ox's giving it an almost prehistoric appearance; and the Pit Bull, even bigger than Excaliber, with canines the size of track spikes hanging from the front of its ugly mug.

Stone felt the pure power of the dogs as their wills tried to take over the wills of the men and the dog. They weren't like normal dogs. Their eyes, black and dilated, seemed to burn with an almost supernatural flame, as if the animals could see right into the men's brains, their hearts. Stone had always prided himself on having a will as strong as any man's. He hadn't broken even under torture, which he had had the misfortune of running into more than once on his travels in the brave new world. But this was something else. He could feel his mind being pulled by their eyes. The blackness was drawing him forward the way a black hole pulls the very planets into its core. Then a voice was telling him to rise, to come forward, to join the animals. And yes, it seemed like a good idea, to just stand and jump down and play with them. They had so much fun together living wild, racing through the rain, lightning flashing in their eyes, the blood of game running down their jaws. Yes, join them, join them, rise and—

"Stone Man," a voice was yelling right in his ear. "Stone Man, don't look in their eyes! Tear yourself away! They can hypnotize. You hear me, man, snap out of it!" It was Cracking Elk, his face just inches away. Stone shook his head. It felt as if he had just swallowed a chaser of LSD or something, as if his brain was being sucked right through his skull.

"Jesus Christ," Stone whispered, pulling his gaze away from the animals, whose eyes blazed as they tried with every bit of the mysterious power that ran between them, that had enabled them to make virtual slaves of every dog on the shoreline, tried to get the three beings above to bend to their will. Yes, it was the eyes. When not looking at them, he could still feel the darkness pulling him, but it wasn't nearly as strong. Stone glanced over at Excaliber, who had walked to the very edge of the ledge and was engaging in his own mano à mano with the Three.

And he was holding his fucking own, Stone saw with amazement. The animal had opened its own oriental eyes to their fullest as if trying to hypnotize the Three itself. With the two humans turning away from them, the Three concentrated all their power on the pitbull. But lo and behold the dog was able to fight it all off. As a representative of the human species Stone felt a little ashamed that he couldn't even do what the dog seemed able to. But the Indian as well couldn't face the combined gaze, Stone reminded himself as he tried to rationalize it all.

The Three sat as motionless as sphinxes back on their haunches while all the other dogs lay around them silent as fallen leaves. The troika just kept staring up at Excaliber, and he met their gaze like a missile sent out to intercept a whole fleet of them. Stone swore he could feel the sheer energy in the air whizzing back and forth. It was almost tangible, yet by a human not touchable at all. There were realms that man would never penetrate though his machines could peel back the very atoms of the universe.

After a good hour of this the Three suddenly turned at once and disappeared within seconds into bushes thirty yards off. Excaliber hadn't flinched. The other guys had blinked first. Stone felt a funny kind of awe for the dog that he wasn't quite sure he liked. He had already had moments where he wondered just *who* was the master in the human/dog relationship. And now the animal's willpower, its pure force of soul, the flame that burns like a fire in every living thing, had proved stronger than any of them, human or devil dog combined. Both men looked down over the great flood of dogs that still remained, all frozen in place, every one of them staring straight up at the ledge.

"The demon dogs, they are the dark ones that the Hawk Dog threw out of the heavens," the brave said in a fearful whisper. "Only the Hawk Dog himself is supposed to be able to withstand their wills. Yet—your dog—he—" The brave seemed confused. He didn't really believe, or want to, that the pit bull was in fact the mythical dog returned from the misty past to fulfill his destiny.

"Oh, he's just a fucking dog," Stone said, getting annoyed at all this Saint Excaliber bullshit. "He just happens to be one of the most stubborn sons of bitches around, so when three ugly mutts try to stare him down, Excaliber won't let them just out of plain orneriness, not because he's the dog from another planet. I mean, give me a break, will you." The damn animal already had such a high opinion of itself that Stone didn't want to give another drop of encouragement to its narcissistic tendencies, or its head might swell so much it would explode in a storm of fur shrapnel.

But if Excaliber was the Chosen Dog that everybody was getting so excited about, he didn't seem to show the class befitting his station. For he suddenly raised his leg and released a quick shower on a half dozen or so collies and spaniels sitting below. Then, satisfied that that about summed up his feelings about the entire situation, the pit bull turned, ran over to Stone, and barked three times as if to say "rock climbing was fun, now let's get the picnic going."

There was no food, no water, nothing, which didn't seem all that terrible to Stone at first. But after it grew dark and still there was no stirring from the lines of motionless animals below, he started getting a little edgy. He needed water, not just to drink but to wash down his still throbbing leg. However none was forthcoming. Cracking Elk, hiding himself from Stone's view as he apparently wanted his Indian secrets to remain just that, did some voodoo over near an overhang that formed a small cave and presto, a small fire was going, with twigs and the whole side of a dead branch that had fallen from above onto the ledge. There was no food, but at least fire. Fire to keep away the cold, the damp, and the dark spirits that seemed to fly above the audience of flesh-eating dogs.

Stone had just gotten himself stretched out on a nice hard, cold piece of rock, bullshitting himself after about an hour of attempts that it actually wasn't too bad and would be just fine to fall asleep on, when the howling started again. Every one of the suckers down there suddenly rose up as if the conductor had just tapped his baton. They opened their jaws, threw back their heads, and howled. Hound dogs and pekinese, chows and sheep dogs, newfoundlands and bulldogs, every fucking breed Stone could remember seeing in his entire life all crooning up at the three fugitives—a death song of love. Such hits as "Let Me Kiss You with My Teeth," and "I'd Love to Rip Your Face Apart," and even "Kidneys Taste Better at Night." All the tunes from the carnivores' top ten list.

But just so the dogs didn't think they were getting away with anything, Excaliber counterattacked with his own collection of Oldies but Goodies. "Fuck You, Fur Face," "We're Coming Down Soon to Kick Booty," and "You Up Front with the Cropped Ear—Your Ass Is Grass," were some of his selections. In any case it made sleep completely and utterly impossible for Stone and the Indian, who just lay there tossing and turning as if their skins were on fire as they endured an endless night of howling and baying from two-hundred nineteen dogs all trying out for the Canine Corps of the Mormon Tabernacle Choir.

When the sun rose slowly as if not wanting to have to endure the sounds any more than the humans did, the battalion of killers was still at it, untiring, taking long slobbering breaths and then letting out with howls, growls, and drawn-out bays that would have made the Hound of the Baskervilles retire. How the animals' jaws didn't tire out and go slack as flat tires Stone couldn't even begin to imagine. But the dogs just kept it up, into the morning, then the early afternoon. Stone and the Indian couldn't even talk above the roar of the crowd, but gave each other disgusted looks every once in a while. How long could it go on? Under the influence of the Three, the army below seemed ready to slash their own mouths to ribbons just to keep up the sound attack. Stone wondered what it would be like to die of dehydration or to be howled to death.

The howling continued right into the evening as Stone could feel his mouth puff up, his stomach expanding like a piece of cotton fluff as his body screamed, begged for water. And with the river roaring by just a hundred feet away it started driving them all mad with a ravenous desire. Suddenly, out of nowhere, the Three appeared again, trotting along at their own swaggering pace. They walked to the front of their army and growled and yowled out a whole set of incomprehensible dog orders. Immediately the entire crew jumped up and shook themselves off after their nearly twenty-four-hour siege of the ledge. Then without even looking up, as if they no longer cared, the Three turned and moved off again at half speed, their tails pointing in the air like sabers behind them.

The entire pack, in no particular order, more a ragged crowd, shot after the departing leaders, jockeying for place in the hierarchy of the band, trying to get further up in the stampede, closer to the Three, as proximity to them conferred status. Within minutes, they were gone, even the last struggling little poodle with a missing leg that skittered along on just three, falling down every five or six steps like a broken wind-up toy.

"What do you think?" Stone asked as he listened on the wind, and heard not a bark nor a howl.

"Trap," Cracking Elk sneered back. "No question about it. You see what those top three are like. They're smart. Never seen no dogs like that. Probably went to plan something. But over? No way. You know it, Stone Man, as much as I."

"Then let's make our move now," Stone said. "I don't want to die up here, puffing up like rotting fruit from lack of water. It ain't the way a man should go. I say we make a dash for the fucking river. It looks a little less flooded. We might have a chance. I know we don't up here."

The Indian paused reflectively to consider what Stone had said and then nodded. "You're on, white man." Stone could see just the vaguest hint of friendship glimmer for a moment behind the dark, savage eyes. After all, when men share imminent death together, it makes for feelings of closeness. The guy standing next to him might well be the last bastard he'd ever see on the face of this earth. But just as quickly the light was out in the brave's eyes and the pupils returned to mirrors, as impenetrable as the slate clouds that moved past overhead. Hearts pounding like jackhammers, the three of them scrambled down the side of the cliff. Then moving like a racing relay team of the insane, they stumbled, lurched, ran, and fell as they desperately tried to reach the river before an army of teeth reached them.

# CHAPTER

# Seventeen

OF course it was a trap. They had gotten only halfway to the river when the whole raging pack, raising up a dust storm like Attila the Hun, came charging in from their left flank. Fortunately for the fleeing trio, the dogs had pulled back a little too far, underestimating how fast terrified humans can run. But it was close. As fast as Stone flew along the rocks and sand, he could feel them coming in from the side, like missiles bearing down. He didn't dare look, knowing that if he faltered for even one second it was all over.

Then the river was just yards away, and as he rushed toward it he felt the crutch he had been scrambling along with suddenly catch in a gopher hole, and he started to topple over and down. But instead of letting the stick do him in, Stone used the momentum of the branch to launch himself forward and up so that he literally flew over the last eight feet of shore. Two dogs flew right by his air currents, their jaws snapping tight. As Stone hit the water, with still fairly slow currents along the banks, he saw Cracking Elk about ten yards ahead starting to float downriver. And splashing around about thirty feet out, also just sort of spinning around in the slower waters, was Excaliber, his head bobbing up and down like a brown-and-white cork.

A few of the dogs tumbled in after them, but the majority stopped at the shoreline barking up a storm, again infuriated at having been so close and yet so far away from satisfying their craving for human flesh.

Those who followed quickly gave up their pursuit as they found themselves tossed around like twigs in the currents. It was impossible for anything without flippers and tail to control its motion in the crazy quilt of currents. Suddenly the pursuers, far from pursuing, were just trying to hang on as they headed back to shore paddling madly. Stone saw two of them disappear under a large wave. The dog pack had already started following them along the shoreline, barking and snapping from about seventy-five feet away. They ran fast, jumping from rock to rock, then running hard along the stretches of clear sand as the river started pulling their would-be dinners faster and faster downstream.

But Stone wasn't paying attention to the dogs. He had his own problem to worry about—like not drowning. As much as he had wanted to get to water just minutes before, now that he was in it and had satisfied his physical thirst many times over, Stone wished he could take a raincheck back to the mountain ledge. For he could hardly keep afloat. He reached down and ripped the splints free from his leg. It might rebreak the damn thing, but with the leg all stiff and useless he had no chance at all. There was no sense in trying to swim, the currents were running the show here. And he couldn't go back to shore, as the pack was keeping pretty much of a pace with them.

But not for long. Within minutes as the three of them were whipped around a sharp bend in the river, Stone could see that it was bad in the boiling stretch that rushed ahead for about two miles. Suddenly he was in a world of bubbles, everywhere white reaching for him, grabbing him, taking him down into its depths with liquid arms wrapped tight around his chest and waist. It was only his physical strength that enabled him to resist the inevitable forces of nature, the watery jaws that grabbed at him again and again.

He couldn't even see the rest of the world now, not the pursuing dogs on shore or his own comrades. Just white caps of foam that kept smashing at him. The hardest part was keeping aware which way was what, so that when he paddled hard after each little whirlpool swept him down, or a wave flapped him straight up in the air like a pancake and he dropped down deep on the return, he didn't swim in the wrong direction. Because, as pilots experience when flying through clouds, you quickly lose the sense of which way is up. Stone found himself spun around, upside down, all over the fucking place. He tried not to puke, though why it even mattered out in the middle of this great toilet bowl, he couldn't imagine.

Suddenly he saw rocks straight ahead. He was being rushed toward them at what felt like the speed a fastball approaches a bat. Stone threw his arms straight out in front of him. They might break, but rather them than his skull. But with the capriciousness of all rivers, a swirling wave suddenly grabbed hold of him and pulled him to an abrupt stop so that he just lightly banged against the rocks. Then he was off again sharply to the left moving through the water as if a shark was dragging him along in its jaws. Suddenly he was just deposited into the slower-moving waters along the shoreline, thrown back like a catch the river had investigated and no longer wanted.

Stone caught his breath as he managed to tread water in the quieter currents that tongued along the shore. There were no dogs, at least none that he could see. But there was a figure, Cracking Elk it looked like, lying in the dirt as if asleep. With his heart pounding hard from fear of what he would find, Stone managed to kick and paddle his way the fifty or so feet to the bank. Then he dragged himself ashore, moving along like a wounded animal, as without his crutch that's pretty much what he was. He reached the rocky shore and looked both ways. This could be a trap too, though the river had been sweeping them along so quickly he didn't see how any of the dog pack could have gotten here ahead of them. No, the dogs had to be miles behind.

Stone reached down and grabbed a stick, much smaller than his previous one, and used it like a cane to move along. He moved forward, his face growing paler and paler. For the body lying there *was* Cracking Elk, and there was a pool of blood gathering beneath his face, which was buried in the mud. Stone reached the body quickly and kneeled down next to it, turning it over fast. He almost gagged. It was the brave, and his throat had been torn right out of his neck, as if a grizzly had just taken a big bite. Arteries, nerves, all kinds of stuff just sort of hung out of the Indian's throat.

But as Stone stared, he was even more horrified to see that the man's eyes opened to half mast and looked up at Stone with that same stoic look that he had had when Stone first laid eyes on him. The Happy Hunting Ground was about to get one cool customer. The mouth of the dying Indian tried to say something, but only bloody bubbles spurted out from between the lips. Then Stone felt the brave's right hand clutch his with a fevered jerking motion. He felt something pressed against it and looked down. A lighter, a windproof Zippo, pressed into his palm. So that's how the bastard had been lighting the fires. So much for secret Indian fire magic.

Stone looked down at the bloody mess of a man and gave him a razor grin. And he swore that through the blood, and what had to be incredible pain, the brave grinned back. Then his lips spoke one final time. And Stone heard the single word, spat out in blood-soaked breath. "Friend."

"Yeah," Stone answered softly, taking the lighter and gripping it tightly in his hand. "I am your friend, pal." But the Indian was dead before he had finished speaking. A stream of blood came out of the opened mouth as if it had one more word to say, but never would. Stone, still gripping the dead brave's hand, placed it back on his chest. Then he closed the staring eyes. Whatever he was seeing now, he didn't need these to see it.

# CHAPTER

# Eighteen

THEN Martin Stone saw that the whole damned thing had been a setup from start to finish. He had been led or pushed like a rat through a maze. For the Three, the trio that ruled the whole bloody show, were standing there, waiting for him. They had run on ahead before the whole circus started, guiding Stone into the water to be pursued by the rest of the dogs, knowing that the waters grew deep and slow here, that the fugitives would come ashore one by one. And the Three would finish them off as they had done the Indian. He had put up a good fight. The Labrador was bleeding from a deep gash along its chest where the brave had been able to wound it with his machete before the Pit Bull had come in behind him and ripped out the whole side of his neck like a piece of cotton candy.

And now the second one with the wounded leg: they would take him next. Ah, the amusement was over too fast. The Three who ruled had been bored lately. They ruled their little kingdom, twenty miles of the river shoreline, like a harvesting ground for anything that was unlucky enough to stumble along. But the animals hadn't had a challenge, something to get their juices flowing, in a long time. They had thought perhaps Stone was the one. But as he sat there on one leg, hardly able to run as they closed in for the kill, they could see that that was not the case at all.

Stone searched frantically around for the brave's machete and saw it lying there on the other side of his twitching body. He started for it, crawling over his fallen traveling companion, but not fast enough. The Doberman shot forward, launching itself from a good twenty feet away like a screaming artillery shell of foaming teeth ready to take his heart out.

Suddenly from the right, moving with equal if not greater speed and certainly more ferocity as his lips were pulled back and a horrible high-pitched sound was erupting from his throat, shot Excaliber. The pit bull slammed into the Doberman's chest at a ninety-degree angle, snapping his teeth around the cords of muscle, the bone, whatever was waiting to be bitten. Both dogs tumbled from the air like two geese who had forgotten how to fly, and rolled around on the ground in a snarling blur of teeth and flying fur.

Stone took the extra second the pit bull had bought him to crawl toward the blade. Just hefting it in his hands gave him a shot of adrenaline. Between him and the pit bull they might just be able to wreak a little havoc. The Labrador took his shot at Stone, taking a running start and shooting up off the ground with legs the size of a rhino's. The sucker was big, maybe 250 pounds heading up to 300. It looked more like a bear or something, but the shape of the face and body structure was pure Lab.

Not that Stone was planning any detailed anatomical charts of the descending canine. He ripped the two-foot blade up, straight at the hurtling shape, at the same instant pulling his body to the side. The animal took a deep cut along its flank and a six-inch-wide streak of red coated the animal's thick black fur. The dog landed past Stone and turned on a dime. If it was hurt it didn't seem to know it. With blood soaking right down to its feet, the Labrador let loose with a most intimidating snarl, spreading its jaws to gargantuan proportions. Stone looked over at Excaliber, trying to face off both the Doberman and the Pit Bull as they circled around in front of him, trying to confuse him.

Stone suddenly had his own ass to watch out for. The Labrador shot forward, coming toward him like a lion at a wildebeest. He tightened his grip around the machete and set himself on one knee, waiting for the animal to come to *him*. He knew that standing up, with just one leg, he was a dead duck. But at least down here he was centered, could perhaps get a good thrust in with the blade. Of course he couldn't get out of there for shit. But he'd worry about that later. The dog came charging at him like a bull, the great jaws inside the black-furred face open like a steam shovel trying to take out a whole fucking skyscraper at once. Stone half closed his eyes and thrust forward with all his might. The blade was ripped from his hands and he threw his face to the ground, covering his head as he rolled to the side, so if the thing started biting on him he'd at least protect his eyes.

But when he dared look after rolling three times to the side Stone saw the dog lurching backward away from him, with the long Indian knife sticking clear through its throat and coming out the back. The dog looked peculiar because the blade had entered so cleanly and poked out at just the right angle, so that it looked for a moment silhouetted in the moonlight, like a horn that had grown a little low. But though the animal stumbled around making all kinds of howls, the damned thing still wouldn't die. Stone knew it would be only seconds before the crazed carnivore would come at him again. Only this time he didn't even have a blade to defend himself with.

Excaliber had his own paws full just ten feet to the left. The attacking Pit Bull circled around him one complete time and then shot in for the kill. It was as if Excaliber was looking at himself, a mirror image coming right at him. Yet the pit bull knew that his opposite number was just as deadly as he was. He wondered if the animal would use the same tactics as well. And as he dove down toward the killer's legs he saw that the other dog did the same thing. They met jaw to jaw, their chins scraping along the rocky ground. The pit bull had finally met his match—a dog that moved and thought exactly as he did.

Excaliber knew he had to be careful with this dude. The slightest miscalculation, the slightest misstep and it would be all over. He pulled back sharply so the attacking bull terrior snapped wildly at the air for several seconds, its eyes closed like a shark, not even realizing that the would-be victim was gone. Excaliber lunged toward the Pit Bull in the second or two it took the animal to get its bearings. He didn't want both the Pit Bull and the Doberman on him at once. It was going to have to be fight and move, fight and move. Because if they both got him at the same time, both sunk their jaws into his body at the same instant, it would be instant death. The pit bull, as tough as he was, was also a realist. And he knew his only chance was to stay on the offensive and keep attacking *them* before they could do the same.

Suddenly he hit like a striking fist and snapped down hard on the Pit Bull's right leg before the animal could do anything. Bite and move, bite and move, he fought like a pro boxer, using the tricks, the feints, everything that his breed had in their repertoire. Again the Pit Bull closed in, coming in fast. Excaliber waited until the last possible second, then dove down under the animal's chest. He stood up suddenly, helping the attacker to get airborne, so it slammed into a tree about eight feet behind him, cracking its head into the hard wood with a resounding bang. But pit bulls are not known as the iron-headed dogs for nothing. The animal merely picked itself up, snarled a few times just to remind itself what it was, and then came charging back again at Excaliber.

Stone watched from the side, with a respite of a few seconds while the Labrador turned for yet another attack, the machete buried through its throat. He knew that he and Excaliber couldn't go on like this for very long. Something would have to give, and what would give would have to be them. Even if they could hold off this crew the rest of the pack would be here pronto. And then they wouldn't have a snowball's chance in a microwave of getting out of there.

Suddenly he felt the lighter in his hand. He was still holding it tightly in his left hand—hadn't let go since Cracking Elk's death grip deposited it there. Stone had a sudden crazy idea. It had only a chance in a thousand of working. But then he didn't have a hell of a lot to lose. He swept his eyes across the Three. They were all off to one side with the mountain wall at their backs about thirty feet behind them. All around their feet were low, dried bushes. Yes, it could work. There was only one fucking way to find out. Stone waited another second or two as he saw Excaliber charge toward the two snarling attackers who were crouched down readying themselves. The pit bull's feint pushed the two back, and Stone saw that at least for an instant they were all together near the mountainside.

"Excaliber," Stone screamed at the top of his lungs as he flicked the lighter and held it to the brittle brown grass about knee length all around him. The lighter caught the first time and the dry brush caught in a flash. He moved ahead a yard keeping the lighter going and touched off another mini blaze, then another. Within ten seconds there was a whole wall of fire sweeping straight toward the mountain wall.

"Excaliber, jump, you bastard, jump!" Stone screamed, seeing that his plan was working only too well as all four dogs were trapped behind the rapidly moving curtain of orange and yellow. The pit bull stopped his battle growling and mouth snapping as he saw the Three staring over his head. He turned, and seeing the wall of flames and Chow Boy on the other side calling his name, did what any good pit bull would do—he dove right into the wall of fire. With his eyes shut the animal emerged on the other side and Stone grabbed him, throwing the animal down in the sand, rolling and half kicking the dog around to put out a few sparking places on its fur where its hide was on fire. But within seconds they were extinguised, and Stone turned to see what his scheme had wrought.

The plan had worked perfectly. The Three were trapped as the tidal wave of fire, leaping up six, seven feet in the air, swept toward them. They backed up howling with terror right to the edge of the mountain wall, and then tried to climb up the side. But it was too steep, their paws only clicking against the rock with loud scratchings like finger-nails dragged across a chalkboard. The wind suddenly gusted and the flames moved right to the dogs like a tsunami of yellow death. The animals screamed out with sirenlike shrieks as their pelts caught on fire.

The Labrador with its full mat of hair went up like a gas tank, just blazing all of a sudden as it shook violently. The Doberman and the Pit Bull followed close behind. Suddenly both of them were flaming as well, the tails first, then the ears, then the whole bodies, burning, burning bright like an Ntani in the night. They joined together in one deafening death howl audible to other creatures miles off, making them scurry back to shelter in their nests and burrows.

Then it was over. Fire is as quick as it is painful. The Three were still upright, their burning carcasses standing where they died, skeletons now visible as the outer layers burned to charcoal and then exploded into hundreds of blowing sparks that filled the stiff wind.

Stone didn't have time for self-congratulations, for he heard a sound and looked up to see the whole fucking inva-sion force of mutts, all of them barking and snarling up a storm like the goddamn canine cavalry coming to the rescue. But it wasn't his rescue.

"Come on, dog, we're taking another bath. And to tell you the truth I don't particularly care if I drown this time," Stone said with disgust as he dragged himself to the river's edge and started wading in like an old man setting his toe into the tub to make sure it's not too hot. The pit bull stood on the bank for a few seconds looking at the advancing ranks now only fifty yards away and coming in hard. He thought about how many he could take out, and decided not all that many. The dog too jumped straight into the river as if it was practicing bellyflops for an upcoming contest.

Within seconds they were both moving out toward the center of the river. The dogs saw their flaming masters and raced along the shore, howling out their anger and fear. What would they do, what would they be without the Three? The Trio had ruled them for years now. Many of the pack had known only their leadership. Already some of the dogs that had stopped in their tracks were eyeing each other, wondering what the hell to do next. Fights started breaking out all along the shore as the glue that had held the pack together began dissolving.

But Stone had other things on his mind than the contractual dissolution of a pack of dogs. For as the river whipped them forward with increasing velocity, he swore he heard a sound like a jet engine ahead of them. Stone wondered if somehow someone could have gotten hold of one, though it was hard to believe that there were even runways to handle a plane like that anymore, or men still left alive who knew how to pilot them. But as the river suddenly whipped him and the dog, floating about twenty feet away, around a bend, Stone saw that it wasn't a jet at all. Ahead was a great curtain of steam and mist rising up high into the sky hundreds of feet. And the roar wasn't coming from above but from below.

It was a waterfall—one of the biggest Stone had ever seen—that just seemed to drop forever as if they had come to the very end of the earth and below were the mist-shrouded lands of another world. A great dark arching rainbow a good mile long curved over the dropoff. It damn sure was a beautiful sight. If you were a newlywed, that is. But if you were Martin Stone and traveling pit bull, it was just about the most horrible thing you had ever seen in your lives. Especially since the two of them were heading right toward the falls.

# CHAPTER

# Nineteen

I T was as if Stone were looking down over the edge of the world, into the fountains of the origins of life. They roared and pounded below him like a thousand dragons breathing foam and uttering screams that pealed across the sky. There was a vast lake below into which the falls emptied, and Stone could see as he looked down that the smashing blast of water churning up the lake for several hundred feet looked as if it could grind metal into scraps. There was no way, no way on this merciless planet that he was going to survive.

As he got to within about thirty feet of the lip of the falls, Stone felt the river speed up with a sharp pull. He could feel his head snap back as his body was caught in the inescapable grasp of the final drainlike currents. And then he was out there, shot out into space so that for a few seconds it seemed as if he might fly, just hanging up there with the lake below and the falls all around him, the dark clouds rubbing across the sky as if trying to steal the patina of the stars.

Then he wasn't flying at all but shooting straight down like a piano dropped from a twelve-story building. He felt remarkably calm as he descended, even turning his head around to see if he could spot the dog. He couldn't. Then he was hurtling into the foaming waters boiling below like a thousand lobsters cooking. He hit hard, not quite aimed at the right angle, so that his chest and broken leg took most of the blow, creating a huge splash that rose for a fraction of a second above the ten-foot-high wall of foam and bubbles everywhere.

Stone felt himself churned around in the crushing floor of the falls like something being whipped into butter. There was no way he could even begin to control his direction. He was ripped every which way, bobbing around like a bottle. Stone had no idea which way was up, or for that matter quite who or where *he* was, as the shock of the fall had knocked half his brain cells into silly putty. He dimly knew that he should be getting some air about now or it was all over. Some air, some air. He really did need the stuff, you know. But when he opened his eyes all there was was water. As if the whole fucking world was made of it. And then, though he knew he really shouldn't, Stone opened his mouth and sucked in hard, just hoping that somewhere in all that water there might be a bubble or two of oxygen for him. And even as the water rushed into his lungs to fill the vacuum created, Stone knew that after all the murderous bastards he had faced and taken out, he was about to be done in by a few quarts of water.

When Stone awoke he was looking into the face of a hideously fat and ugly angel. He knew it was an angel because he had to be dead after his descent to the bottom of the falls, and because the face was completely white and pure, dressed in white, with white hair and white skin, white lips. But he had always believed angels to be beautiful, and this one was something that would make the creature from the black lagoon have stomach problems. The skin was all bloated, dripping with oozing sores and boils everywhere. The eyes were red pinpricks that seemed suited more to a rodent than a man or an angel. And the teeth, the rotted black stumps that filled the blubbery lips, looked as if they had all been pulled out, ground up, and glued back in again at any old angle, because they sure didn't fit right.

Even as Stone, in his dim-witted state of consciousness, tried to figure out just how God could make something so mismatched, so repulsive, he swore he was seeing double.

For suddenly appearing right next to the first was a second virtually identical face. And its lips were moving.

"Time to wake up. Time to wake up." Stone knew he was in heaven now because that was exactly how his mother had always awakened him in the bunker. Was this what his mother had turned into in heaven? Then he wasn't in heaven, he was in hell. And as his head cleared slightly and Stone managed to push himself up to a sitting position he realized that he was in a much worse place than hell. He was on earth.

And he was looking at two of the most repugnant specimens of humanity that had ever popped out of a womb. As his vision cleared Stone saw that there *were* two of them, two obese monsters, with not radiant satin-white skin but rotting, pockmocked albino flesh. They were total albinos, white like chalk, like long-rotted meat, like the larval mucous shells of maggots. And they were fat. Jesus Christ, had these two packed it in. They looked like hardly more than heads atop great round snowballs covered in the filthy, bloodstained clothes that draped over them. The men must have weighed something approaching a half ton between them. And Stone swore, as his eyes seemed to come back into total focus, that they were identical twins. They both had the same ratlike features, the red junkie eyes like blood on the tip of a needle, flaccid cheeks hanging down around their faces like the jowls of a diseased rooster. No necks at all, just those shapeless lumps atop much larger shapeless masses.

They smelled too: bad. For the mouths laughed—or something that was supposed to be laughter—and the smell that emerged from both pairs of lips reminded Stone of something horrible. But even as he reached for the memory in his mind, one of the foul mouths spoke up.

"You don't look like an Indian." The lips hardly moved, as if the white blob of a face had a hard time exerting the energy to work them.

"I'm not a fucking Indian," Stone cursed, the question making him angry for some reason. Suddenly one of the albinos reached out with a fat arm, fingers as white as a servant's gloves, and, grabbing a piece of flesh around Stone's upper arm, pinched hard. Stone pulled back, slapping the hand away.

"What the hell do you think you're doing?" he shouted. "Keep your fucking hands off me. I may be down, but I can still cause plenty of damage."

"Just testing for your fat content," the albino mouth answered in reply. "Not too good—your fat-to-muscle ratio is very low, just like the damned Indians."

"Listen, I don't know what the hell you fellows are talking about," Stone said, trying to sound a little more friendly, "but whatever it is—and I thank you for saving me, if you did—really I've got to be on my way." He tried to rise again, wanting to get the hell out of there as fast as he could and find the damn dog, if the creature had survived the fall. But everything just didn't seem to be working the way he wanted it to. It was as if his nerves were short-circuiting from the near drowning, and his legs suddenly collapsed under him when he was only halfway up. Stone fell back onto the ground thrashing in futile anger.

"He's got a lot of life and that's good," one of the albinos said. Stone had trouble telling them apart except for the fact that one's voice was about an octave higher than the other's. "Makes the meat sharper tasting, perhaps will add the spice that the lack of fat will mean."

"No, no, I don't think so at all," the other answered, sounding quite depressed, as if he'd been disappointed yet again. "He'll just be like leather. I know it. Nothing to sink your teeth into, just a lot of chewing, and spitting out half of him."

Stone didn't like what he was hearing, to say the least. He hardly allowed himself to believe what the words implied. Surely they were playing with him. This was all some kind of sadistic game. He found himself a little less dizzy after collapsing on his side and raised his head up again, this time keeping his body flat on the ground, like a baby taking its first crawl. And he didn't like what he saw. For there were a lot more of them than he thought. There must have been a good dozen of them standing around in a rough semicircle. They were equally foul-looking and clothed in tatters, almost subhuman appearing with dumb, scarred faces. Drool dribbled from their open mouths as the hairy faces just stared like cows. The obese twins who had been addressing him were, Stone saw, sitting in large metal wheelbarrows side by side, which were being held and balanced in back by two men holding onto each handle, the handles reinforced and extended with metal L-braces to support the elephants inside the barrows. The cavemen types who had been pushing the albino brothers were still wiping the sweat from their foreheads though they had put the two down many minutes before.

"What the hell is going on?" Stone asked angrily. He didn't like being toyed with, like a mouse by a cat. "Who are you two bastards?"

"The second question first," the one on the right replied, his thick legs draped over the front of the wheelbarrow like huge loads of thick white dough about to be baked. "We are the Hungry and these are our people." He waved his hand around to include the whole motley crew, all of them so pimple ridden that Stone wished he could have had the Clearasil franchise for the area. "We are so named because, as you can see"—he patted his huge stomach—"we are always hungry."

"I am Top," the other one spoke up, "because I like the meats from the top, you know—brains, the heart, the lungs, and of course, the eyeballs."

"And I am Bottom," the other rotted egg spoke up with his higher-pitched voice from the other wheelbarrow, arms resting on the sides like overstuffed pillows. "Because I prefer those meats from the lower portion of the animal."

"And as to what is going on," Top said with a laugh, so Stone's eyes shot to the closer of the albino brothers, the edge of his wheelbarrow only inches from Stone's face, "it's really quite simple. We're going to eat you as we do all those who fall into the river, Indians mostly. And as my brother says, they're not very tasty. But you, we'll see. With a few spices, some oregano, some bat feces to bring out your natural flavorings, I think I can do wonders." He smiled at Stone as if the future roast should be equally happy about his gastronomical fate.

"Listen, you fucking slime," Stone screamed out, filled with an uncontrollable rage at hearing all this talk of cooking and flavoring. He tried to rise again, ready to strike out any way he could at the bastards. But even as he grabbed hold of the edge of the closest wheelbarrow and, pulling himself up, began trying to pound the face of one of the albino cannibals, the army of subhumans closed in from all sides. Baseball bats, shovels, lead pipes all swung out of the mist-splattered haze, the roar of the falls like a thunderous drum behind them. It wasn't exactly the most aesthetic of attacks. But then when it comes to bashing in someone's head it doesn't take a lot of finesse.

The last words Stone heard before he felt something smack into the side of his head and his brain going back and forth like one of the bells at Notre Dame was, "Watch out, you assholes, don't bruise his flesh." Then he was a bloody Peter Pan flying mad circles in Never-Never Land.

## CHAPTER

# Twenty

WHEN Stone came to, he was bouncing up and down, his hands and feet tied tightly, inside a wheelbarrow. How nice of the cannibals, Stone thought absurdly as he came out of his throbbing black pit of a brain, to give him a ride. He was in the center of the marching band of squat and muscular maneaters, all walking along like the fucking seven dwarfs. Only they had already eaten Snow White and they were hungry for more. Ahead of them he could see the two brothers in their own souped-up wheelbarrows being pushed along by grunting teams of underlings. They were arguing, though he couldn't quite make out the words, about just who was going to get what and just how he should be cooked, neither of which was very soothing to Stone's ears. Maybe the damned dog had been better going out the fast way in the falls than having to go through what Stone was about to endure: being eaten. The animal had been too proud in life to have been able to stand that. Its heart would have broken, and hurt even more than the pierced flesh. And suddenly Stone found a small and dark happiness in the fact that the animal would not have to endure this.

When they reached the edge of the albino brothers' camp Stone wished that *he* had perished in the falls too. For the sight was as sickening as the most nauseating photographs he had seen of the Nazi Holocaust. Bodies were everywhere in all stages of rot and decay. Bones littered the ground from the moment they came into the square the size of a city block that the slime bastards had cleared and called home. The place looked like the garbage dump for a slaughterhouse. Only *these* bones were all human, the skulls those of *homo sapiens*, with twisted grins of terror set forever on their ivory faces. Half-eaten slabs of dessicated meat lay stacked in piles as if for later snacking, while arms with hands still on them were hanging in a line from a pole, drying out in the little bit of sun that peeked down through the charcoal gray clouds. The albinos had discovered that they didn't even need to tie the arms up, just to curl the fingers around and the rigor mortis held the things in place as if they were holding on to the straps on a subway train.

As the caravan of albinos, caveman dwarfs, and Martin Stone passed deeper into the camp, Stone saw the rest of the "tribe" walk out from their hovels to inspect the newest catch of the day. They walked stooped over, with animallike expressions on their faces. Spittle hung from many mouths

as they jumped up and down hungrily. The inhabitants of
this quaint little cannibal town looked as if they belonged
back in Cro-Magnon days rather than in twentieth-century
America. They hardly looked human.

As some got too close and reached out toward the wheelbarrow Stone was riding in, the brothers Albino let loose
with snaps from long horsewhips that they pulled from
within their foul flesh-coated robes. The half-humans
snarled and pulled back, loping along, their hands almost
touching the ground. What a fucking place, Stone thought,
shaking his head back and forth in disbelief. The depths to
which the human race could sink never ceased to amaze
him.

Then he saw that it was even worse than that. For as the
half-humans ran from the whips of their masters, Stone
squinted through his swollen eyes and saw that the round
structures he had at first taken to be some kind of tents were
in fact just that, except their coverings, which consisted of
twenty-foot strips attached over branch frames, were made
of human flesh. It was obvious because the builders of the
wretched structures had left the hands, fingers, knees, and
feet all pressed into the dark, taut material. Everything was
still there like a rich man's bear rug in front of the fireplace
with head, tail, paws all intact. Just the flesh within, all the
muscles, bones, and slime, had been removed, then the
quarter inch or so of actual flesh was dried out in the sun
until it achieved a leathery but somewhat flexible hardness
that was perfect for all-purpose weather protection. When
stretched tightly around their frames the human skin structures kept out rain, wind, snow, sun. Stone saw as they
passed close by one that the dwellings weren't exactly sewn
together by master craftsmen but more thrown together any
which way with thread made from the dead humans' own
intestines. They were like immense purple-tinted canvases of
the dead, creations of a macabre colony of artists with a bent
for the darkest visions of the human soul.

The wheelbarrows moved right through the center of the
camp, and Stone saw that with the exception of the albinos

everyone else in the place was of neanderthal appearance. The brothers ruled through sheer terror, force of will, and superior intelligence. For the dumber but stronger half-men could easily have killed and dismembered the two—what a meal that would make. Yet they shrank in fear in all directions as the food procession moved along, like long beaten dogs skulking off from their hard masters. Stone's nose sniffed deeply a few times almost on its own as if it were a separate beast. Then he gagged. He could smell the cooking human flesh in the air. He had smelled such a scent before. He'd had run-ins with flesh-eating scum before. Only then his Harley 1200 had been functioning as had all its weapons systems: .50 cal. machine gun, 89-mm missile launcher, and various other tricks and treats. But now he had nothing, not even the fucking dog.

Stone's wheelbarrow passed a long trenchlike fire that had been built into the ground. They were apparently trying to get a whole ten-foot length of flaming wood reduced down into glowing red coals, and the subhumans tended the fire like a steel mill requiring constant attention, running back and forth along the fire line, poking at the burning timber with long pieces of metal rod to get everything going just the way it should be. Trained by the brothers, they moved with the automated mindlessness of robots, enjoying their simple-minded work but not even comprehending why they were trying to make the coals. And standing next to the fire, awaiting their turn to be roasted, were two bodies. They were naked, throats slit, genitals already sliced off. And they were skewered with long three-inch poles from mouth to anus, the poles slammed right through the centers of the bodies and then into the dirt so the two were facing straight down, their heads about a foot from the ground, two-hundred-pound shish kebabs ready for the grill.

One of the subhumans was coating the bodies with some sort of sauce, no doubt a concoction of the albinos', since these half-naked creatures were clearly incapable of even mixing spices together, but only painting them on with an old paintbrush in long, even strokes, trying their dumb best to get every square inch of the slowly rotting flesh, marinating it just right for the evening's feasting.

Suddenly the procession came to an abrupt halt, and Stone swung his head around to the left where the brothers' carts were being circled. More human game, only these were alive, a woman, a young man, and a much older fellow, still distinguished looking with white beard and tortoiseshell eyeglasses. They were all tied to stakes that had been driven into the ground about two feet apart. They didn't look happy.

"Here we go," the albino named Top said as his and his brother's wheelbarrows were swung around right in front of the poled captives.

"Now take *him*," Bottom commanded the halfwits who came toward Stone, lifted him, and carried him toward an empty pole next to the woman. When he was all tied up and hanging there, as if standing on his feet like the others, the brothers had themselves wheeled back a few yards to survey their four treasures.

"Well, we'll save this batch for tomorrow night, what do you say, dear brother?" the high-pitched voice asked as he rubbed his pasty hands in gleeful anticipation. "We should really finish up that pair by the cooking fire. They'll rot beyond all digestibility if we leave them even one more day."

"Yes, yes, I agree," the other replied. "These four will make a fine feast to celebrate the founding of our village three years ago. Why, perhaps we should even have them live. You know the juices are so much tastier, the meat so much tarter."

"Why, I think you might be right, brother," the other said, leaning over from his wheelbarrow so he almost fell out. "We haven't had live meat for so long. Usually the meat is in such dreadful condition. But these, these . . ." He sat back with a happy look on his fat, rotting-dough face and signaled with a hard bang on the side of the steel barrow for his team of subhumans to push. With a collective groan they raised the back end of the thing and started forward, the other albino's cart following close behind. They had their teams push them over to the two corpses that were pierced with the poles and began berating the marinater severely.

"No, you fool, stroke the brush from *bottom* to top, *bottom* to top," the higher voiced albino squealed. "How many times do I have to tell you brainless worms!" He pulled out his whip and gave the subhuman a vicious whipping, snapping the leather whip out again and again until the cro-mag's whole body was wrapped in red welts, bleeding lines. He howled like an animal and dropped to the ground, covering his face with his hairy arms, shaking and trembling. After about a minute the other brother blurted out from his own barrow.

"Enough, dear brother, you'll kill him. Their kind taste terrible, you know that. And it took us nearly six months to train the turd even to do as well as he does. The others you'll remember couldn't even learn to keep dipping the brush into the special sauce. I can't bear the thought of having to train another of the brainless dogs."

"Yes, perhaps you're right," the first said, snapping out one more stroke just for good measure and then pulling the whip back to him, wrapping it into a coil and secreting it under his bloody coat, once a long white physician's robe, now greasy and splotched with the remains of his many dinners.

"Bottom to top, bottom to top," the other albino screamed out to the quivering subhuman, who had sat up and was sort of looking through the cracks of his fingers like a child watching a horror film. The brother moved his hand in a long slow motion, making a charade in the air as he lay slumped back like a diseased egg in the wheelbarrow, trying to show the fool how to do it.

"Ahh," the de-evolved once human croaked as his eyes watched the up-and-down strokes of the albino's hand. "Ahhh," he intoned again, getting a big smile on his cracked lips as if he had just understood some great revelation, although it had been demonstrated to him a hundred times before. But aside from being nearly as dumb as cows, the other feature of the tribe was their inability to remember anything for more than a minute or two.

"Oh, the tools we have to work with are just deplorable," the brother who had just whipped the drudge spoke out with a depressed sigh. He slapped the side of his barrow again and the four cro-mag's raised it fast this time, after viewing the whipping of their own. The second brother followed along behind.

"We all have our crosses to bear. And this is ours, to be saddled with an army of men with the brain power of amoebas."

"Yes, but is it not through this very suffering on our parts, the constant wear and tear on our nerves, that we in fact grow and are challenged. Was it not Nietzsche who said, 'that which does not kill me makes me grow stronger.' I think, dear brother—"

"Oh, but brother," the other cut him off as he snapped out with the side of a shovel at one of the subhumans who had drawn too close to his wheelbarrow. The shovel nearly cracked the creature's head in two and it rolled on the ground screaming, hands over its suddenly red-coated scalp. "Was it not Hegel who stated that evolution, growth to a higher spiritual reality comes only through the *overcoming* of the obstacle. Thesis, antithesis, synthesis. Why, it is the way of all things. Yet you seem to believe that *we* should be excluded. That our meaning lies in suffering and not in achieving a higher, more perfect plane—"

"Brother, brother," the other exclaimed with an exasperated laugh. "Once again you twist my meaning from its Platonic ideal into a most vernacular vulgarity. All I meant was . . ." The two albinos had been having this basic argument about the ultimate meaning of man's manifestation on earth for some twenty years now. It was never resolved but just continued endlessly on, like an old clock making its repetitive tick-tocking rounds.

"No, I think you're quite wrong on this point," the high-pitched brother squeaked, starting to grow angry though they had the same argument at least a thousand times before. "I think we must consult The Books."

"Yes, the Books," the second agreed enthusiastically as he shifted his weight in the wheelbarrow like a huge snail turning over inside its shell. "The Books shall tell us. The Books."

They rode at a half gallop, whipping at their teams behind them as they bounced along like shipments of white sausage back to their own human-skin homes in the center of the camp, up on a rise about ten feet above the rest of the place. They headed to their Books, a collection of treatises and sets of the great writings of philosophers throughout history. The Books contained all knowledge, all truth. Human flesh and ultimate knowledge, what finer mix could there be. The wheelbarrows were pushed right up the pathway of the round dirt mound atop which their home was constructed. The subhumans pushing them could hardly make it up the steep grade and looked as if they were about to have heart attacks as they stumbled but dared not let either wheelbarrow go over. They knew the consequences. Somehow they made it to the top and pushed the barrows right through the hanging flaps of human skin which slapped back together again once they had passed, like the dead things that they were.

Stone shook his head in disgust, realizing he had been half hypnotized by the presence of the two. He turned his head to the right and gazed right into the eyes of a *real* angel. The girl was beautiful. She couldn't have been more than twenty, with the kind of face that men would have, and had in past times, killed for. She was staring straight at him with tears running down her cheeks. She sniffled hard and tried to speak but seemed to only be able to stutter incomprehensibly, so traumatized had she been by all that had befallen her recently.

"Easy," Stone said softly. "Easy." His own flesh hurt like hell, though the way they had tied his hands up and behind him helped support the weight of his body. Still the broken leg had been banged around like a fucking basketball and it felt as if razors were slashing along the inner nerves. So it was sort of nice in a weird way that there was such a distraction as a beautiful woman only inches away from him, their shoulders and hips almost rubbing together.

"Now slowly," Stone said, smiling at her to try to make her relax even a little so that she could talk. "Who are you? What happened to you all?" It worked, for after taking a deep breath the woman spoke very slowly, enunciating each word carefully as if it were a torture to even relate her experiences.

"I'm Charise. Charise Gordon, and this is my—my brother and my father." She turned, with her head looking toward the young man who was tied to the pole on the other side of her. He was slumped down, out cold with a nasty gash along the top of his scalp. Beyond him the old man looked just sort of dumbfounded by it all though he didn't appear badly hurt. Stone snapped his gaze back to the woman and encouraged her to go on.

"We—we were trying to flee from our town about fifty miles south of here up to Canada, where we have relatives. It's much better up there they say. Not as violent, not as horrible. My t-t-town was wiped out by a gang of bikers. They came through like stormtroopers raping, burning, not leaving a trace of our homes or the families that had lived there for over a century. We—my family and I just got out in the nick of time in our jeep." Her eyes darted from his face to a spot across the encampment and Stone's eyes followed. He could see the shape of a vehicle covered with a tarp about two hundred feet away on the far side of the place.

"We—we were about five miles from here just going down a road—when they—they—" Her eyes filled up again as if a storm were about to fall. "They attacked us. Suddenly they were just everywhere, dropping down from the trees. My brother fought back and they hit him hard with a club. I think he's—he's dying." The tears started falling.

Stone let her cry for a few minutes as he looked over at the young man, leaning forward in his own bonds to get the right angle. The guy's whole head was cracked. She was right. Without treatment he was dead. Maybe even with it. Not that any of them had a very long life expectancy.

"What about your father over there?" Stone asked after she had stopped and began wiping at her face with her shoulders.

"He's—he's—I don't know what's wrong with him. But ever since the attack he's just been in a daze. Oh—I—" She started to break down completely, Stone could see it.

"Easy now," Stone said, "it's not over till the fat lady sings, you know what I mean?" He whispered out of the corner of his mouth, though he instantly realized that none of the subhumans who were walking around the camp bent over carrying bodies and parts of bodies were able to understand more than a fraction of what he was saying. They didn't even appear to care what he said, being more concerned with not fucking up their tasks and getting the shit whipped out of them by the albinos.

The expression, a remnant of old America, made her grin for just a moment through the tears. But it was enough to break the spell of total doom. She smiled at Stone and it made his heart skip a beat and something start stirring in his loins, which he couldn't believe. He was amazed that in a camp full of cannibals, tied to a post, with his dog dead, his leg broken, and his ass about to be turned into meatloaf, he still could find the time and the energy to get horny.

After about twenty minutes, just as the sun fell and the coals burned down for good cooking, the albino brothers emerged from their human-skinned two-story tent and were wheeled back down to the picnic grounds. The two corpses were lowered on their stakes over the fire and placed sideways onto long turning devices, sort of like the spits chickens used to spin around on, dripping grease, in the windows of delis and supermarkets. The scent of cooking flesh drifted over to Stone and the girl and filled their nostrils with the nauseating aroma of charred man. And thus they had to spend the entire evening smelling and hearing the two psycho brothers chomping away on organs and arms, while they vociferously argued the finer points of the German philosophers of the nineteenth century.

# CHAPTER

# Twenty-one

AFTER the slime had eaten and argued until about two in the morning (Stone could tell the time by the star patterns above, which his father had drilled into him in their years in the bunker), they retreated back to their little skin castle on the hill, burping and farting up a storm. Stone couldn't sleep, to say the least, nor could Charise, though her father dozed off like a tired old professor standing and giving a classroom lecture about nothing. Once she saw that the albino twins had left and that most of the cro-mags were asleep out in the open, their arms clasped around bones or human heads like children's teddy bears, she whispered over to Stone again.

"I'm scared, Stone. I just don't feel brave at all. I don't want to die. I don't want any of us to die."

"Any man or woman who said that they weren't scared shit right now, they'd be a liar," Stone replied with a soft whisper. "I'm scared too." He looked at her and tried to smile, to show her that at least one person on this fucked-up piece of rock called earth was not a murdering cannibal. And she seemed to feel something, for she brightened and returned the smile, her eyes glowing like little stars.

"Tell me, Mr. Stone," she went on, glancing around to make sure they weren't being overheard or observed, "do you—do you believe in God? In an afterlife? Do you think we will go anywhere when we die, or just into those grotesque stomachs?" She seemed nervous as she spoke, her long red hair flowing about her neck and head like a cape of fiery wheat. But once the questions were out, a look of relief settled over her face as if it had been important just to ask them, to release the thoughts that had been preying on her mind like a lion on a carcass for the last thirty-six hours since they had been captured.

"I think yes, we will go somewhere beyond just the digestive tracts of the albinos," Stone said, looking her hard in the face. "I mean we already were nothing, came from nowhere, before we entered these bodies, didn't we? We once didn't exist already. Out of nothing, into something, back to nothing again. As far as I can see we'll re-emerge again in some other form, human or not, I don't know. It's not something I can prove, just a feeling but a strong one. Sometimes when I'm very tired, or relaxed—or drunk—and lying down somewhere so that there isn't a bit of tension in my body..." Stone stopped as he suddenly felt for an instant how incredibly tight all his muscles were right now, as if he had been wound up tight as a steel coil and was ready to explode.

"Anyway," Stone went on, "when I *do* feel relaxed, I swear I can feel that I was something before I was this. There are dim memories in the back of my mind, images that are almost but not quite there. Do you know what I mean? It's as if there's a curtain over the past before this life. It's something we're not supposed to see or understand. But that doesn't mean it's not true." Stone stopped suddenly, feeling a little embarrassed that he had delivered such a monologue. He hadn't even quite realized that he had had such feelings, beliefs, before. But imminent death stirs up deep waters.

"Thank you," Charise said after nearly a minute of silence

as she continued to look deeply into his eyes like a faith-
starved saint staring madly up into the pillowed clouds of
heaven searching for God. "Thank you for sharing that feeling with me. It means more than you can know. To feel that
there *is* something more, something beyond. I have dimly
felt such things too, but couldn't put the words to them like
you did. I don't feel as afraid of dying now," she said, with a
determined look on her beautiful young face.

Stone couldn't help but glance over suddenly at her right
breast, which hung out exposed from the shirt that had been
torn somewhere along the line during her capture. The breast
was as perfect a specimen as Stone had ever seen. Like an
exquisite golden fruit rising out as if to catch the rays of the
sun, rising to be warmed and plucked. He tore his eyes
away, suddenly realizing he had been sort of spacing out
right on the pink nipple, and coughed as he looked away.
Torture turned to desire. Fear to lust. Man was a strange
creature.

The milky rays of the moon bathed her long golden-red
tresses. Silky flesh raised on milk and butter and honey,
upturned erect nipples, smooth turn of thigh and arm,
slightly flushed rosy-cheeked face. Stone felt his groin swell
and throb with a sudden urgent, insane desire.

She began crying again and Stone turned to her, wishing
more than anything that he could hold her, comfort her, kiss
her.

"Don't cry, sweet Charise." But he couldn't really offer a
reason not to cry. Even if one *did* believe that there was an
afterlife, leaving this one in the teeth of those albino slugs
was enough to make even the toughest of the tough sick to
his stomach.

"Stone—they plan to use me tomorrow." She winced in
pain at the very thought. "Earlier today, before you came,
they were touching me all over and laughing about how
they'd construct a pulley system to lower me on top of them
since they were too fat and didn't have the strength to do it
their filthy selves."

"Jesus," Stone muttered with a sharp intake of breath.

Somehow his whole little rap seemed like so much bullshit in the face of her words. Being raped by those two might be worse than being eaten by them. She looked at him hard now with the burning fire of the half-possessed in her blue-green eyes. Her expression was strange, fearful, and curious.

"There's something else. I—I—am a virgin. They will—I don't want it to be this way. I may be dead within twenty-four hours—but first they'll rape me, both of them, perhaps even their filthy servants." She looked down at the cold, hard earth, hardly able to continue. But her own rising desires were stronger than her natural female shyness. She raised her head again. This time her eyes were bold, flaming like novas. "I want *you* to take me first. A decent man to be the first one into me, to make love to me."

"I—I—" Stone stuttered over and over, tongue-tied like a buck-toothed thirteen-year-old on his first date. "It's not that I wouldn't be honored, don't get me wrong," Stone said, looking around to see what the cavemen were up to, but every one of them was out cold. Not a figure was stirring. "But we're not exactly in the best situation to—" He looked over at her brother, who was hanging there still unconscious, and her father out in the land of Nod, perhaps never to come out of it. A fun bunch to hang out with.

"I have my own ways," she said. "Watch!" She squirmed suddenly at her bonds, pulling her whole body this way and that, wriggling her extremities like a belly dancer, so that she was able to stretch her lower torso all the way around—and their bodies were hip to hip, though their heads were still about two feet apart. He felt the ice-hard erection swelling under his zipper as she lifted her foot and undid the pants, then the zipper. He looked at her in amazement.

"We used to have contests in high school to see who could perform various tasks with their feet so we could see what it was like to be handicapped to have no arms or hands. I was the best." Stone could see that she was, and just what a useful talent it was. She opened his zipper with her right foot, pulling with her toes, and the engorged member burst forth.

"They never thought of this," Charise said with a sly smile, massaging the tool with her foot, running her sole up and down the shaft, curling her toes around the organ so that Stone instantly started going half mad.

It was really quite amazing what a shot of male hormone in the bloodstream would do for one's energy level. For though Stone had felt he was ready for the morgue just minutes before, now, with her half-naked lushness, the triangle of hair between her legs exposed like a golden fleece, he suddenly felt as if he was ready to go fifteen rounds with Muhammad Ali. Though a few minutes with the woman who was pressing hard against him would be far preferable.

"Do it," she said frantically. "Please, Stone, help me somehow, to get it in." She sounded half mad, with the look of the fanatic in her eyes, to lose her virginity, and fast. She gripped one leg around his waist and pushed up hard with the other. She pressed the moist lips of the furry triangle forward until it met the swollen head of Stone's manhood. She was wet, very wet, and giving off a scent that made him feel intoxicated, the scent of fruits and flower petals and musk and the inside of a woman's creamy thighs. She pushed her hips forward, trying to find him, spasmodically reaching for him with her center, again and again. Tomorrow she would be dead. She would give her all, her love, her body to this man, at this moment. There would be nothing else.

"Please, do it, get it in," she pleaded, her eyes rolling back, her whole body starting to tremble. Stone guided the probing staff in by moving his hips. Suddenly the very tip of it reached her and slid in between the parting flesh lips.

"It's hard, it hurts," she groaned, a single tear falling down each of her flushed cheeks. He pushed suddenly with all his strength to penetrate her, get it over with fast. She gasped and rolled her eyes heavenward as the organ moved suddenly, cleanly into her. She froze, motionless for a second, trying to get used to the newness of it. Then she began moving, slowly at first, up and down on the long shaft, then with increasing vigor and jerking motions, holding on to his hips with her right leg wrapped tight around his hips and back. He slid in and out of her in deeper and stronger strokes, filling her whole center, her stomach. She moved against him like deep velvet being cut by a knife, like a girl/woman who had realized her dreams at last, even in the very midst of death.

"Stone, Stone," she mewed, like a deer calling in the soft grass. "It's so good . . . it's . . ."

"Don't talk," he said, "they'll hear us. But I know, I feel it too. Your body is—is paradise." Then they were both reaching that peak called orgasm, a series of quivers the first signs from her; the relentless buildup of a bull-like load, of a Hoover Dam about to burst, sent shudders through his tortured body. Then they came, simultaneously gasping out, heaving in jerks of complete ecstasy.

At last their tremors both subsided and he slipped out from her as she choked down a scream of loss. "I love you. Can I say that, Martin Stone? I know it's insane, completely mad. But can I say it just for this night?" He stared back at the beautiful creature beside him.

"Always," Stone said as softly as he had ever spoken in his life. "Say it always."

"Tomorrow when they come, they'll find a woman. A woman who has already known a man. They can do what they want with me now—because I don't care. They can take me but not dirty me."

He looked at her with tears in his own eyes now. Because *he* did care. Suddenly he cared terribly what was going to happen to her. He couldn't let her die, which meant that he had to save himself, save them both, no matter the impossible odds. Stone had touched her perfect beauty and he wasn't about to let it die.

# CHAPTER

# Twenty-two

THE only thing worse perhaps than knowing he was going to be eaten in a few hours was the fact that Stone had to listen to the two albino brothers arguing with one another all fucking day long. From the moment they emerged from their human-walled tent on the hill that morning they were snapping at each other from their respective wheelbarrows. Arguing about which plates they were going to use tonight, about how to roast the meat, about whether to have some of them as appetizers or all as the main course. In a world of narrow parameters the brothers found plenty to fight tooth and nail over.

They spent the afternoon preparing their sauces and spices that they were going to use on the four prisoners. But though the sauces got made the arguments and snipping at each other only grew fiercer as the day wore on. One of the subhumans made the unfortunate mistake of spilling a whole vat of some precious flavoring or other right into the coals. After they whipped him to shreds they had his head bashed in and then threw him to the other cavemen to eat. The subhumans tore into the bloody burger oblivious as to whether they were eating their own kind or not. All meats digest the same as they pass through the stomach.

Stone went half crazy when the two wheel-barrowed loads of sludge had themselves pushed over to their four prisoners. They had their underlings strip them all completely naked. Stone strained at the cords that held him securely to the pole, wishing he could cover Charise's nakedness from the slime bastards. For the moment however all they wanted was to baste the four. Two vats were brought up and their neanderthal servants, the more intelligent of the lot, were set to work slopping the foul-smelling "sauces" all up and down them, covering every inch of their bodies. Stone felt humiliated, infuriated to the point of exploding. It was worse than being whipped, beaten even. Denying him even the dignity of being a man, turning him into nothing more than a meal, a Sunday pig, a goose, a hanging duck in a Chinese deli.

"You bastards, you fucking slime bastards," Stone screamed over and over uselessly as he lunged out, trying to kick at the two.

"Ah good," one of them laughed out so that every part of him shook and shimmied like some diseased jelly. "That's excellent, yell, kick, do it all, it increases oxygen in the blood, makes the meat tastier, much tastier." This of course only made Stone even more furious so that he turned red and leaped straight up in the air, throwing out a side kick at a ninety-degree angle.

But of course they had positioned themselves out of range of their prisoners. In the past their captured "dinners" had often lashed out when tied up—the albino brothers had the scars and missing teeth to show for it. Not that much of anything was distinguishable within the folding drips of fat that were their formless faces. Just fat white lips that moved and argued and directed their slaves to "be more fucking careful with the bat guano, you fools." All in all it was just about the worst afternoon Stone had ever spent.

They were to be eaten when the sun went down. Or at least the meal would begin. For the four of them were to be spread out between sundown and midnight. The brothers debated every detail of the banquet, either not caring that their "meals" heard every word of their fates, or more likely enjoying the sadistic mental torture as well to the hilt. Stone was a mental wreck trying to figure some way out of all this. He couldn't allow it to happen, not just his own death alone, but all of them eaten by these slime. It just couldn't be. And yet try as he might, searching every brain cell that still functioned, he couldn't find a single fucking route of escape.

If his wrists had been tied a little bit looser it was possible. But the bastards knew their fucking knots. For as much as he squirmed, pulled from side to side, ripped his wrists at the leather thongs, he couldn't get them loosened even a fraction of an inch. Cannibals apparently had their accessory skills. What would the fucking major have done? Stone tried to imagine his old man caught in this situation. But he never would have allowed it to happen. Probably wouldn't even have allowed himself to get caught in the fucking landslide in the first place. But try as he might to conjure up the major's image in the fading light of the day he couldn't, no face appeared in the clouds or rose from the flames. Stone was alone, unutterably alone, and he had no way out.

Then it was dark. Just like that and the two white slugs came over in their wheelbarrows. Again they argued, snapping and snarling at one another like an old couple married forty years, about who should have the honor of being the first meal of the evening. Stone kept his cool this time. He knew he'd need every ounce of strength. He'd make his move when they came to take him. There'd be dozens of the subhumans around but he'd have to try.

But it wasn't Stone or the girl whom they chose first. Rather her still unconscious brother, who the brothers agreed, after twenty minutes of vicious screaming catfight, had to be the first since he was closest to death and they didn't want to lose any of their precious fresh meat. The young man was cut down and loaded into a third wheelbarrow. Then the entire procession was wheeled over to a blood-splattered wooden table as Charise screamed and screamed again.

"Roger, Roger, please God no—don't take him. Oh no, no, no." But there wasn't a thing she or Stone could do about it. Her father stared out blankly as if looking at infinity. The cro-mags took the naked body, now coated with orange and green creams and sauces a half-inch thick, and threw it right up in the center of the table, which Stone could see even from a distance, by the flames of the cooking fires off to one side, was covered with blood and a thick, oily dried slime of the past bodies that had been consumed on it. The bastards had their own picnic table, half-broken umbrella above it and all. A regular family fucking outing.

As Stone and the girl looked on in horror they saw that the slime weren't even going to cook Roger. They were going to eat him alive. The albinos had their underlings push the wheelbarrows they were riding in forward and up to the table, one on each side so they were facing each other. Then the cro-mags tilted the wheelbarrows forward, holding the things up at an angle using their shoulders to keep them upright against the great weight pushing down on them. The albinos reached greedily forward from across the table, and each holding a huge kitchen knife sharp as a razor, dug right into the still living, breathing, though mercifully unconscious man.

Charise gasped as a long red gash appeared across his chest and stomach. Then they reached in and ripped out still-beating organs, squirming pancreas, rippling kidney, and popped them right into their mouths, chewing and laughing lustily over the fine taste. Then she couldn't look and only Stone remained staring at the dreadful sight. They cut into the living youth again and again, as they plucked his eyeballs from his head, digging them out with olive tongs and popping them down whole, like fresh clams.

Stone watched as they cracked open the skull with large calipers and argued over the brain, fighting for it with their hands, grabbing at it so the mass of pink stuff just dissolved between their fingers and squeezed out onto the table and down to the ground. He watched as they sliced open the chest and again fought over the treasure inside. But one stabbed the other in the arm and reached in quickly, grabbing the still beating organ.

"It's mine, you turd, we agreed last week: you get the brains, I get the heart."

"But you TOOOOOK the brains," the other screamed

back hysterically, licking at what little of said substance it could from its fat white fingers.

"Well, too late now," the high-pitched voice squealed as its hands pulled hard and ripped the heart right out of the youth's open chest cavity, trailing tendrils and veins and all kinds of spurting shit. The albino held it and looked at it as one might look at an exotic species of jungle bird. Then he bit into the thing even as it kept beating, jerking spasmodically away from the broken teeth. But the heart, to say the least, didn't have too many defenses, and the cannibal tore into it with gusto, taking huge, still beating bites of it, which flopped around like fish as they swam down his gullet and into the festering lake of his huge stomach filled with rotting foods from days past.

Stone watched while every square inch of the youth was carved into an unrecognizable bloody carcass like a turkey left over from Thanksgiving dinner. There wasn't going to be a hell of a lot to munch on come midnight. But then Stone realized they had more to eat. Much more: him.

It had been dark about an hour, and the brothers albino were just finishing up the last of what had been a man, when Stone suddenly sensed, felt something behind him in the shadows. He turned, moving very slowly, though the brothers, nearly a hundred feet off, their faces covered with blood as they chewed out the marrow from the bones, were hardly in a position to notice him.

"Jesus fucking Christ," Stone hissed under his breath. It was the dog! The fucking dog was alive and it had come to save his ass. The animal looked curiously out of the bushes, somehow sensing that it shouldn't come rushing ahead barking and tail wagging and everything. Stone made a shushing sound with his mouth, a signal he had tried in the past to make the pit bull understand meant play it cool, boy, real cool. The dog slithered around the dirt like a snake and came right up behind the stake Stone was tied to. It let out a low guttural growl as if asking, what next?

Stone wriggled his hands tied behind his back around the pole and whispered, "Bite rope, dog! Bite the fucking ropes, you hear me?" The animal put its wet nose close to where Stone was wiggling and seemed to poke around there like a hog rooting for vegetables, trying to figure out just what the hell he had in mind.

"The rope—bite—the—fucking—rope," Stone said very slowly and deliberately, as if talking slow would make it all a little clearer. Somehow, it did. For the animal, suddenly realizing that the ropes had something to do with the Chow Boy's predicament, nuzzled up close, standing up on his hind legs and opened his jaws about an inch. Moving in close and making sure that he was only getting leather, not flesh, Excaliber closed the teeth slowly until he made contact with the material. Then he grunted and snapped hard with all the strength of his breed's jaw, over two thousand pounds per square inch. Even leather cord as tough as this wasn't meant for that kind of stress. The cord snapped apart in the pit bull's mouth and it pushed back down, landing on the ground with a soft thud.

"Stay," Stone ordered out of the corner of his mouth as he pulled his hands partially but not all the way around just to make sure they were completely free. They were. He looked over at Charise, whose eyes were closed, her head turned sideways, not able to bear to look at the remains of her brother.

"Charise, baby," Stone whispered sharply out of the corner of his mouth. "Listen to me, you've got to snap out of it. I've gotten free. I'm going to try to make a break for the car. Now I've got to know. The machine gun you told me about, remember?"

Her head suddenly snapped up out of its daze and she focused on him. "Yes, the machine gun—"

"Is it loaded? Did they take the feed away or leave it all there? Is the thing operable?" Stone prayed what the answers would be. For with them lay their only chance at getting out of this foul-smelling nightmare alive.

"Yes, yes, I think they just left everything," she replied, her eyes suddenly burning with a touch of fire as she realized what was going on. "I was conscious the whole time we

were brought to camp. I remember them looking at it and
then saying they would worry about it later. They had to eat
one of the other men they'd caught before he died. They just
threw the cover over it, that's right, yeah, covered it with
that tarp, but didn't touch a thing. I'm sure of it. But how
did you get free?" she asked as she saw Stone swing his
arms around from behind the post.

"Can't talk, baby. Before they get hungry again, I've got
to make my move," he replied. "All right, come on now,
dog," Stone hissed in the darkness. "If you're ever going to
earn your keep"—which he knew as he said it had never
been much—"now's the fucking time. You're going to have
to run interference for me to that car across there." Stone
shut up. The dog didn't need a fucking scorecard. Everybody was the enemy. It was easy.

He pushed himself off and forward. Which was all well
and good except in his excitement Stone had forgotten he
had a broken leg. He got about two steps, the dog darting on
ahead snarling and baring its teeth, when he tumbled onto
his ass in the dirt.

"Great!" Stone snarled at himself in supreme humiliation.
But even as he hit the ground he was up and moving again,
hobbling along on one leg. Just ahead of him, moving
through the encampment carrying a long pole with empty
water gourds over her shoulder, was a bare-breasted hairy
cro-mag female, heading off to get water so the brothers
albino could wash down their recently chewed repast. Stone
slammed his knee up out of the darkness before the woman
even knew what hit her. He felt bad about hitting a woman,
but not too bad, especially when the excrement-smelling,
hairy, low-browed, toothless hag he sent into sleepyland
looked as if she should have been in *Return of the Ape
Woman* instead of carrying water in Colorado.

Stone grabbed the stick and slammed it down into the
ground right up against his broken leg, making a stiff sort of
instant splint. Now he could move, he found out after just a
few lurches forward. And once he saw that he could, Stone
didn't look back. The dog had cooled its snarling in the

darkness, waiting for Stone to get his shit together. When it saw the Chow Boy coming out of the flame-flickering darkness like a maniac ready to kick ass, then the dog was ready too. It opened its jaws wide and the two of them took off side by side. They had to move right past the cooking fire next to the cannibals' table. It was dark now, the cooking fire being allowed to burn low, for apparently they planned to charcook everyone else.

But he hadn't gotten halfway across the open ground when the shit hit the fan. A group of five of the cro-mags dragging over a huge cooking spit from storage saw the two of them and let out a screaming chorus, jumping up and down to alert the camp. They threw their load to the ground and came forward on all fours, broken teeth bared like animals. Stone shuddered but he didn't stop. Timing himself so he was on his good leg he brought up the stick he was holding and slammed one of the subhumans right under the jaw. The sucker flew straight up into the air and then stumbled backwards. Even as Stone's foot came down he swung the stick back to the ground to help catch most of the force.

The dog tore into the next man who was trying, stupidly, to block the way. Stupidly because when you stand in the way of a charging pit bull without a bazooka to take it out, you make a big mistake. The slave futilely swung at the dog with a bone club, but the animal merely sidestepped the blow and sank its teeth into the attacker's knee. The whole section of the hairy leg ripped out in a spray of blood, bone and gristle. But the pit bull was already past him and on, eyes darting back and forth searching for the next fool.

Three more of the beastie boys flew into the fray from the left. Stone had to stop completely, balancing himself on one leg as he swung hard in a wide arc with the pole. He caught two of them in the head at once and both went flying. The dog leaped straight up from the ground at the face of the third and caught him around the chin, biting down so hard the man's whole lower jaw fractured into five parts and his face sort of bent in like an accordion. The dog spat out the dripping chunk as it never ate human flesh and was back at

Stone's side as they darted across the encampment. The distance to the jeep, which hadn't seemed that far when he was tied up, suddenly seemed like the fucking Sahara Desert as they tore across it, trying to beat the slowly rising crowd of charging cro-mags. The albino brothers realized something was wrong now and came out of their stuffed semislumber as they heard the screams of their underlings.

"He's free, kill him!" Top screamed as he raised up an inch or two from his wheelbarrow. But the effort, particularly since he had just ingested about forty pounds of flesh, was tremendous, and he sank back down into the wheelbarrow with a loud *thwack* so that the four men who were under and behind the barrow felt their backbones nearly crack under the weight as they tried desperately to hold the thing up.

But even as the foul subhumans came loping from every goddamned place now, Stone and the dog just headed on in a straight line for the jeep. Another hairy fellow jumped from a tree and Stone caught him in the head with his elbow. The man grabbed his forehead, which had cracked like an egg, and fell backward right into the arms of another of his ape-like breed. The pit bull took out a foot, then a knee, then a face in the half light.

At last Stone saw the jeep just ahead, with no one blocking the way. He made a lunging leap and took out half the bones of his chest as he didn't quite make it up onto the side but slammed right into it. Gasping for breath, he pulled himself the rest of the way up and ripped the tarp off the back part of the open jeep. Charise had been right. The brothers, after examining the thing for food and not finding much, just covered it and left it. Where Charise and her family had gotten a U.S. Army issue .50-cal. machine gun mounted on the back was something he would have to ask her about later, if there was a later.

Stone fumbled agonizingly slowly with the feed belt, slamming it into place, pulling off the safety. Thank God he had practiced with the major back in the firing range of the bunker, with just such a .50 cal. His father had stocked the place with only the best. Because if Stone had been even a second slower he would have been a dead man. He slammed the lead bullet into the chamber, resting the feed belt over his shoulder as a whole group of the neanderthals came charging straight toward the jeep waving clubs and assorted sharp implements. He prayed and pulled the trigger.

The muzzle of the mint-condition weapon erupted with a roar of fire, and a load of slugs the size of small birds tore ass out of the steel barrel. The first dozen or so cro-mags were less than ten feet away and coming at Stone like charging rhinos when the bullets slammed into them. The slugs, meant to take out armored vehicles, planes, a small tank or two, ripped into the bodies like a wolf into carrion, shredded the attackers, sending flesh flying into the air in a bloody snow all around the jeep. He whipped the gun all the way to the right, where a large contingent were coming at him like a whole mountain slope full of gorillas, only these gorillas were armed with shovels, picks, and sledgehammers.

Stone pulled hard, feeling the heat of the .50-cal. as it burped out white-hot lead and the whole jeep shook beneath his feet. The subhumans fell beneath the withering fire like so many pick-up sticks being tossed to the ground. They had never seen a machine gun, or couldn't remember from their past lives as human beings what the hell the things were. It was impossible that a single man, Stone, could stop their hordes. And so they kept coming, dying en masse, not even realizing what it was that was doing them in.

Stone heard growling from the back side of the jeep and realized with horror that the half-humans were sneaking all the way around. There was no way in hell he could swing the big .50-cal. around in time. And then as if in answer to unspoken prayers the pit bull jumped from the driver's seat where he had been guarding things and took out two faces, snapping back and forth in the air like a windshield wiper of slashing teeth. Stone prayed the dog could hold back the ranks and concentrated his energy on the ones from the camp. They just seemed to come from everywhere, out of

holes in the ground, out of their human-skinned tents. Stone
sprayed them down, glancing nervously at the box of ammo
at his feet. There wasn't a hell of a lot. Maybe hidden under
the floor of the jeep? But Stone didn't have time to look for
ammo. If he stopped firing for even a few seconds the still
advancing masses, waving weapons and screaming like a
zooful of enraged animals charging from the bloody mists,
would inundate him.

Suddenly Stone saw the two albino brothers being pushed
down a slope toward the jeep. They were each holding a pair
of 9-mm semiauto pistols and were firing like mad as their
teams of savages pushed behind, running as fast as their
thick muscular legs could push the great loads. Within seconds the wheelbarrows built up speed and came hurtling
down at Stone like two battlewagons. The obese albinos
fired away with each hand pulling the triggers relentlessly
from their sluglike positions back in the barrows.

Stone let a dark grin spread across his face as he whipped
the muzzle of the .50-cal. around and got the lead wheelbarrow dead in his sights.

"This is for all the poor bastards you ate," Stone screamed
out, though no one heard above the din of the firing and
the screaming masses. But they heard the bullets rip into
the barrow and tear it into smoking fragments that flew in-
into air. They heard it in the screams of Top as his fat flesh
was torn into chili, exploding out in a torrent of blood that
instantly filled the big wheelbarrow and overflowed onto the
ground and beneath the driving legs of the pushers behind.

Stone's smoking barrel found the other wheelbarrow as
well and its inhabitant. "I'm sure you want to be with your
brother, don't you, slime?" But he didn't wait for an answer.
He pulled and kept his finger on the trigger in a madness of
battle. The slugs tore into the albino and his transport, trans-
forming them into a mixed smoking red mush that flew into
the air as bullet after bullet stirred it around. Within seconds
there was nothing left that was recognizable of the two.
They had been transmuted into the same kind of indecipher-

able hamburger that they had turned Charise's brother into. There was some justice, if little, in that.

After he saw that there wasn't a bit left of the two brothers to fire at, Stone let his finger ease up on the trigger, thinking he should conserve some ammo. There was a sudden eerie silence as the whole battlefield stopped in its tracks and everyone checked to see just what the situation was. The cro-mags realized with both horror and joy that their albino masters were dead. And the fight went right out of them. The brothers were dead. There was no reason to fight anymore. And like the animals that they were, they broke ranks and ran in wild packs into the forests, howling and screaming at the moon, with the strange and exultory realization that they were free.

## CHAPTER

# Twenty-three

"HERE, help me load your father onto the jeep," Stone said, as he pulled up at the aged shawled man, who had gotten only one foot up onto the back and then sort of become stuck. He didn't remember how to do things too well anymore.

"Sorry," Charise said with an embarrassed look as she pushed up at her father's backside, forcing him to move forward into the back of the jeep from which Stone had shot down half the fucking town. He guided the blank-faced man to a built-in steel seat on the side and wrapped the blanket tighter around his shoulders and lap as it was a cold morning, the air thick with a frosty mist that bit into the skin, the lungs.

"Come on, let's split," Stone said, sliding into the driver's
seat. He checked gauges for the fifth time that morning. But
everything was okay, filled to the brim. They had prepared
well before leaving on their journey to Canada. They just
hadn't been able to prepare for fate. Charise jumped up onto
the seat beside him and managed as much of a smile as she
could on this cold, hard morning. Stone reached out and
touched her face.

"Things will be okay," he lied with as much sincerity as
he could muster.

"Sure," she lied back. But that was all there was these
days. Just a forced smile, a word or two of total untruth. At
least it held the spirit from slipping the last inch or two into
dark madness.

Stone glanced over at the grave they had dug for Roger,
her brother. There hadn't been a hell of a lot to work with.
But they had managed to construct a sort of coffin from
wood and buried the remains with all the proper prayers and
rituals they could think of. They didn't bury anyone else.
Not that any but the dead were there to stand wake. The rest
of the subhumans had fled, never to return presumably. Only
the willpower of the albino brothers had held the whole
place together. Without them there was nothing. Just the
rotting carcasses of the dead and the twins' own sluglike
bodies, which formed a large oily sludge in the very middle
of the camp, a spot Stone couldn't even look at.

He started the jeep and it purred to life instantly, thank
God for small favors. But then they owed them upstairs after
what they had just put them all through.

"Come on, dog," he yelled, then whistled hard through
chattering teeth, tightening his own jacket against the chill
wind of the morning.

The pit bull appeared from out of the bushes that led to
the river. It had a flopping trout held tightly in its jaw. The
animal trotted forward, jumping over the bodies, leaping
across mounds of half molded flesh. He reached the jeep and
in a single fluid motion jumped up onto on the back of it and
walked over to the old man. The dog dropped the fish at the

dazed man's feet and then put his paws up his lap and snorted happily.

"I think the mutt likes him," Stone laughed as he turned back around and started the vehicle forward. It moved with a few lurches as he got used to the pedals and the steering, then they eased bumpily forward, riding over rocks and mounds. Charise pointed toward the left in the direction of the road they had been traveling when they were attacked. At last Stone was leaving the river valley. For the first time —in how many days?—he would be out of the claustrophobic claws of the place that he had to endure from the moment the avalanche had kicked his ass.

Still, things sucked, to say the least. All his equipment, everything had been lost in the fall into the river. And his sister, April, Jesus God, what was happening to her? He had been on his way to find her when— It seemed that the more he tried to rescue her from the hell she had tumbled into the further he found himself from her. As if he were on a treadmill that just pushed him backwards.

And yet Stone knew he had not the slightest choice. If he spent the rest of his life searching for her, if he ended up wounded, crawling, his very life's blood spurting out of him as if painting a highway line, still he would go on. For she was all that remained of his family. And Stone knew that without even the possibility of finding her, it would be hard to keep his own damned engines going in this dark, dark world.

He would drive north with the girl, until they got near the bunker, then she'd have to be on her own. For now. Maybe someday there would be room for love. But not on this cold morning. It wouldn't be far to the border. She'd make it. And Stone figured it probably *would* be better up there. It damned well couldn't be any worse.

He would have to rebuild everything from scratch. He knew there was a motorcycle frame back in the hidden mountain retreat, even some extra wheels and welding equipment. The major had planned for every eventuality. Christ, he could tie some fucking smg's onto the bars with wire if it came down to it. It didn't have to look as pretty as his first bike did. Just kill as good. Because God knew there was enough killing to do on the bloody road to save his sister. And anyone who got in his way was going to find themselves floating down a red river.

Stone heard laughter and turned around as his foot eased up off the petal for a moment. Charise was laughing and pointing.

"Oh look, Dad is smiling. Your dog is like a psychiatrist for him. See, he's getting better already." And Stone had to grin along with her, for the dog, its front legs up on the old man's lap, had pushed its face right up to the shellshocked seventy-eight-year-old's face and was licking his cheeks with long wet strokes. First one cheek, then the other. And even her father couldn't stay within his terrified shell with that treatment. He reached up and half tried to push the animal away. Then he laughed. Out of the pale white near-dead face a laugh somehow emerged. And then another as the dumb dog just wouldn't stop licking his face. As if it knew the old man needed healing. And even the tiniest bit of love from a dog might do the trick. And then they were all laughing as the jeep pulled out of the campsite. Laughing almost hysterically and the dog joined in too, howling and growling at the crazy skies. And it was a strange sight indeed, not that anyone was watching, to see them laughing so as they left behind a battlefield of dead who were not laughing at all.